GARDENER

To my mother

THE
GARDENER

SEAMUS DUNNE

Wolfhound Press

First published 1993 by
WOLFHOUND PRESS Ltd
68 Mountjoy Square
Dublin 1

and Wolfhound Press (UK)
18 Coleswood Rd, Harpenden
Herts AL5 1EQ.

Wolfhound Press receives financial assistance from the Arts Council / An Chomhairle Ealaíon, Dublin, Ireland

British Library Cataloguing in Publication Data
Dunne, Seamus
    Gardener
    I. Title
    823.914 [F]

    ISBN 0-86327-392-0

Typesetting: Wolfhound Press
Cover design and illustration: Aileen Caffrey
Printed in Great Britain by Cox and Wyman Ltd, Reading, Berkshire.

Prologue

Heinrich Obermeyer pressed his right foot gently on the spade and it slid obliquely through the soft soil. He tugged at the shrunken stalk, uprooting it and, scattering soil with the spade, disinterred the potatoes. He picked one up and rubbed it on his corduroy trousers and its skin emerged ochre from the clay.

'It is a good crop,' he said aloud, as though addressing a robin which, flaming in the September sun, pecked worms from the fresh earth. He began throwing potatoes into a wheelbarrow.

Heinrich had not always been such a contented gardener. On the surface, he was just another industrialist attracted to the country by low-cost labour and a facilitating government, but in his case a more important inducement was the fact that Ireland, the independent part of it, had been neutral in the war, hadn't fought against, or been occupied by Germany.

At war's end, he had returned to his native town in Bavaria. His parents were dead; his home obliterated. Smoke from the stacks of the Obermeyer factories had guided the bombers. He found accommodation with his Uncle Walter, an able sailor in the political tide, who had navigated the Obermeyer family enterprises through the war. As the *Wirtschaftswunder* started to take effect, Walter offered Heinrich a machine-component factory in Ireland, a ship of his own in the

Obermeyer fleet. Heinrich accepted immediately.

In Fernboro, Heinrich was busy with plans for commissioning the factory. He would remain in his office late into the night, struggling with theories in an effort to understand the origins of the events that had swallowed his youth. Mind straying from tortuous philosophic thoughts, he would become conscious of the silence of the factory which, up to thirty years before, had been a British army barracks. Soldiers had gone from there to France and Flanders; perhaps, Heinrich surmised, to meet death from an Obermeyer grenade.

The Angler's Hotel, his first home in Ireland, was frequented by many of Fernboro's business and professional men, who greeted him courteously, but, as he avoided the bar as much as possible, he was seldom in their company. He hadn't always been a moderate drinker: in one terrible year, when he'd journeyed to the edge of Asia, he had used vodka as an anaesthetic.

———————

When the ends are great humanity employs other standards...Nietzsche's words were blurring on the page for a weary Heinrich one night when he heard a tap-tap on the office door. It was Carmel, his secretary, who had noticed the light in her boss's office as she was cycling home from a visit to a friend. Heinrich's weariness evaporated and they chatted. And, for the first time, he spoke to her about his parents, childhood, and friends.

Carmel Ahern was twenty-three, eleven years Heinrich's junior. His capacity for work amazed her, absorbing her notepads and pencils and typewriter, and she spent hours, many vexatious, on the hand-cranked telephone. She was also an interpreter, elucidating for him the nuances of Munster speech and the Irish way of life. After a while, he began to savour the morning coffee-breaks they shared and to detest more and more his lonely Sundays, the only day of the week he didn't see her.

The Obermeyer factory was officially opened by a government minister, and Heinrich celebrated the occasion by treating Carmel to a film and a meal in Cork. They made the journey in his newly acquired car. He remembered that beautiful May evening: Carmel was wearing a blouse that matched the colour of her eyes and the green of the passing fields and her auburn hair was gold in the light of the setting sun.

Carmel repaid Heinrich by inviting him to her home, where he was regaled with bacon and sausages and eggs, brown bread and butter and jam, all home-produce. He relished the family atmosphere and enjoyed the company of Carmel's father, Jim, and her brother, Peter.

Carmel and Heinrich married the following spring. By the standards of the Irish farming community, the disparity in their ages was not remarkable. People said the young Ahern girl had made a 'good match', and—prime approbation—they noted that Heinrich was a baptised Catholic. Shortly after his marriage he applied for Irish citizenship, and his study of theories declined. He filed aspects of his past in the recesses of his memory; radioactive material in a cavern, but the cavern was fissured.

Their son, Eamonn, was born three years after Heinrich first came to live in Fernboro. When Carmel's parents died, Peter took over the Ahern farm. On average, Heinrich visited Bavaria only once a year to report to his cousin Franz, who had succeeded Uncle Walter as head of Obermeyer Enterprises.

Heinrich rested his chin on his hands that grasped the top of the spade handle. He looked westwards: framed in branches of trees was a majestic four-span stone bridge, Fernboro's architectural glory. Further to the west, he could discern the mountains whence flowed the River Fern.

He wheeled the potato-filled barrow, on which he had placed the spade, towards the house: red-brick, two-storeyed, hip-roofed, twin chimneys, set in two acres between river and road—built a hundred years earlier for the commanding officer of the British garrison. Heinrich, with Carmel's approval, had purchased the property shortly before their marriage.

Closed curtains on an upstairs window caught his eye. He looked at his watch and frowned: eleven o'clock and Eamonn was still in bed.

From the road, came a sound that attracted Heinrich's attention by its rarity—the clip-clop of hooves.

Chapter 1

Mary McCarthy, a child under each arm, legs dangling, sat on the brightly painted flat cart that was drawn along River Road by a plodding piebald cob. Back-to-back to her and the children were seated her brother Ned, reins in hand, and his wife Bridgie. A donkey, haltered to the cart, walked behind it, and to the tail-board was tied a canvas bundle. A greyhound walked alongside.

'This must be the place,' said Ned, pulling the cob to the left. The cart jolted on to a rutted, weed-strewn stretch of ground, a no man's land, between the road and a wire fence.

Mary slid to the ground and massaged her travel-sore bottom. Then she helped Ann, aged three, and Davy, a year older, to alight. Mary was sixteen, the third eldest of nine children. Ned, nineteen, was the first-born and a month previously he had married eighteen-year-old Bridgie.

'I wonder what kind's the quality round here,' mused Bridgie, a peroxide blonde with an open face, as she and Mary untied and removed the bundle from the cart.

'I don't know,' said Mary. 'This is our first time stopping at this end of the town. But I'd say there's real quality in that house down there in the trees.'

They carefully lowered the bundle and unrolled the canvas. From its folds they took food and vessels—their generic name for pots and pans and delf. 'I could do with a cup a' tae after all them miles,' said Bridgie.

'We'll have to get water somewhere,' Mary replied. She too was thirsty: they had been on the road for nearly three days, travelling in stages from a seaside town over fifty miles away, the advance party of the McCarthy clan.

Ned, face and neck red from the sun, bleached hairs sprouting from his freckled muscular arms, unharnessed the cob, unhitched the donkey and upended the cart on to its tail-board, tilting the shafts skywards. He tied the animals to the fence at a spot where grass was plentiful, allowing them enough rope to graze at their ease.

A cattle trough in a nearby field yielded water and they made tea. Then, as the water was plentiful and the day fine, Mary and Bridgie set about washing clothes in a large plastic basin, their arms bare to the shoulders, Mary's deep-brown, her sister-in-law's lightly tanned, pummelling piston-like in and out of suds. They sang along with the country songs coming from Ned and Bridgie's radio-recorder, and in the air was the acrid though pleasant smell of woodsmoke from the fire to which Davy was carrying kindling.

In the lee of a holly hedge, Ned erected two tents, earth-hugging structures, into which all but the smallest child would have to crawl. At least, he thought, me and Bridgie have a tent to ourselves. He wished he owned a caravan, but consoled himself with the belief that a tent was healthier in good weather. When a lot of people were in a caravan, water started running down the walls. Look at what the caravan had done to little Ann: she had been two months in hospital with her chest.

That was around the same time as he was in jail for assaulting a garda. Lots of fellows were in the fight and he just hit out. When he was vexed he'd lash out at anybody, quality or travellers. Something like his father, except that his father would show his anger only to the family and to travellers, and was nearly always nice to the quality, calling them sir and asking them the time.

Jail, the cinema, radio, occasional glimpses of television, and the increasingly affluent lifestyle of the settled community made Ned impatient of the fatalism displayed by his parents. Imprinted on his mind were the words of a traveller whom he had heard on the radio:

After all we are human beings like everybody else. This statement had the impact of a profound revealed truth on Ned who, as though he were a toddler discovering the power of speech, repeated it frequently, *sotto voce* and aloud.

Mary and Bridgie wrung out the clothes and hung them on the fence.

'I'm glad there's no cows in the field,' said Mary.

'Why's that?'

'Do you remember that grand yellow cardigan I had? Well, a cow pulled it off the hedge where I'd left it to dry, and licked it and chewed it and I had to throw it away. The woman who gave me the cardigan asked me where it was. When I told her, she said I was telling lies and wouldn't give me notten else.'

Bridgie sniffed. 'Serves you right,' she said. 'You shouldn't tell the quality notten.'

Tom McCarthy drove his van towards Fernboro, towing a caravan. It was he who had noticed, during one of his numerous trips in search of scrap metal, the idle strip of ground on River Road, and judged it a suitable place for winter quarters: near the town, yet in the country, with access to firewood from trees and hedges, with the possibility of fodder and grazing, and with ample space to store scrap. He hoped that no one had got there before Ned and Bridgie and Mary and the children, whom he had sent ahead a few days earlier.

Tom was thirty-eight. His bushy, wiry, ginger hair, untouched by grey, contrasted sharply with his lined face.

In the passenger seat was Maggie McCarthy and on her lap was the youngest of the family, Kathy, aged eight months. Three other children were stretched out in the back of the van—Paddy, Tom Junior, and Sheila. Lukey, eighteen, the second-eldest of the family was visiting relatives and was to get married shortly before Christmas.

'The young ones do things their own way now,' said Maggie, her thoughts surfacing.

'What're you talking about?' Tom said.

'Lukey—the way he's courting. Not like in our time.'

'We done all right.'

Maggie supposed that they hadn't done too badly. She had first met

Tom only a few hours before their wedding, which was arranged by a matchmaker. She had fancied another lad and he had fancied her but her parents hadn't approved. She was a grand little thing then, only seventeen, raven-haired and slim, like Mary was now. The babies, all the babies, had destroyed her figure and she had grown so fat that nobody knew when she was pregnant and when she was not. Though he gave her the odd clout, Tom was nice enough except when he lost his temper, and he had saved up and bought a van and caravan and she hadn't to lie on the ground any more. She hoped that they would be able to stay in Fernboro for the winter and that the quality wouldn't want them moved.

Tom touched the brake as the van entered the outskirts of Fernboro. He'd make sure to keep within the speed limit. He didn't want to draw the gardai on to himself; the less you had to do with them the better. These days you couldn't piss but you'd land in court.

'Look at that,' he growled, nodding to his left, towards a patch of land that resembled a moonscape: heaps of rocks amidst deep furrows. Nearby was a sign with the inscription, *Welcome to Fernboro*.

'You'd find it hard to get a caravan in there,' said Maggie. It was where they had camped the previous winter.

It's the same everywhere, Tom reflected. Once the travellers left, the Council moved in and ploughed up the place so that they couldn't return. The McCarthys had been on the road since time immemorial, and that's where Tom wished to remain. He liked being able to come and go as he pleased.

He had the dole and sold scrap and dealt in horses and ponies and asses. His father, God rest him, had been a tinsmith but all that kind of work was gone. The travellers always used to be called tinkers but now some of the quality called them itinerants. Knackers was another name but he'd burst anyone who called him that. When he was a boy the travellers had plenty of places to camp and a lot of the farmers would give them grazing for the horses and would have buckets and vessels of all kinds for his father to mend. The rich travellers were a sight to see in them days. You'd hear them coming from a long way off, and you'd see them out of a cloud of dust—most country roads weren't tarred then—big stallions with ribbons on their manes and shining harnesses with bells pulling bright caravans and upright men and women that'd hardly glance at you. Mares followed by loping foals cantered behind the caravans, sleek horses that you wished were yours.

Most of those rich travellers had left the road and settled on farms, but they kept their horses. The younger ones spoke like the quality but he was told that they were often called knackers behind their back. As regards the origins of the travellers, Tom had heard various tales: that they were the descendants of journeying craftsmen, of horse dealers, of people driven on to the road by famine, but the story he favoured, and that he had passed on to his children, was that they were the real Irish people who were forced to wander because they'd been robbbed of their lands by foreigners.

After crossing the bridge, Tom steered the van to the right, up River Road and into the new camp-site. Garments of all colours were draped on the fence, pullovers and cardigans and shirts and blouses drying in the afternoon sun, like bunting heralding Tom's arrival as head of the clan. Maggie stayed in the van for a while, too lethargic to move, and clucked her approval of the bright clothes. She was dressed in a red-and-blue striped frock—a far cry from the days when every travelling woman wore a plaid shawl. She still had a shawl but only used it when she was in desperate need and had to go begging. People seemed to give you more when you were in a shawl, especially if you had it wrapped around a baby as well as yourself.

'Are you going to stop there for the night, woman?' shouted Tom, and the van shook as he and Ned unhitched the caravan. Maggie handed the baby to Mary and heaved herself out.

Mary cooed at baby Kathy. She was accustomed to caring for the younger children, who gravitated towards her like chicks to a hen, and she accepted this responsibility as being only natural. From an early age, travelling girls were mothers in all but the physical sense, and Mary was already passing on some of her responsibility to her sister, eight-year-old Sheila.

———

The McCarthys were around the camp-fire: Mary filling mugs with strong smoky tea and ordering the children to be quiet and not to be grabbing the sugar; Sheila cuddling the baby; Bridgie dispensing sizzling sausages and rashers from a large iron pan; Tom and Ned discussing likely sources of scrap. Chewing on a thick slice of white bread, Maggie laid down the sleeping arrangements: Sheila and the baby would share the caravan with her and Tom; Paddy and Tom Junior would be in a makeshift shelter under the cart; Mary and Davy and Ann would be in the tent.

Dusk thickened. There was a clink of bottles, contented belches, the crackle of burning timber. Tom and Ned grasped pint bottles of porter. Maggie and Bridgie and Mary were drinking cider. Mary poured cider into a mug and passed it from Sheila to Davy to Ann. Paddy and Tom Junior each had a mug of porter which they had inveigled from their father.

———————

Not far from the strip of waste ground, Mrs Helen Moran stood at her bedroom window, her gaze rivetted to the camp-fire. A figure rose, silhouetted by the firelight, and then lurched out of sight. It rematerialised behind a hedge and squatted.

Mrs Moran turned away from the window in disgust.

Chapter 2

Philip Shaw and Heinrich Obermeyer might once have tried to kill each other, or so they had sometimes placidly conjectured. On this Tuesday evening they were ensconced in deep armchairs in the Obermeyer dining-cum-living room, sipping post-prandial brandies.

Seventeen years previously, Heinrich had been introduced to Philip in the bar of Fernboro Golf Club. Major Shaw was then in his mid- to late-forties, sandy-haired, moustached, sufficiently tall to disguise a tendency towards plumpness. Heinrich and Carmel frequently chuckled at Philip's attachment to his military title: they were among the very few people in Fernboro who addressed him by his Christian name.

Through playing golf together—both were more enthusiastic than accomplished—Heinrich and Philip became better acquainted and began to exchange reminiscences on army life. Paradoxically, their acquaintanceship blossomed into friendship when they discovered that they had faced each other as enemies across the Rhine in March 1945. They had been in the same sector near Essen.

The name Fernboro in an advertisement in *The Times* had attracted Philip's attention and awakened a memory: of his mother telling him about the place, of how she and his father had been happy there in the first year of their marriage. His father, a regular army officer—the Shaws were a military family—was killed at the Marne in 1914. Philip's mother remarried and made a new home in India, while he remained in England, in public school, spending his holidays with an aunt and uncle. From school he went into the army.

The advertisement, inviting applications from ex-officers, was for a steward to take charge of what was described as a demesne. Philip felt a sense of alienation from postwar Britain: the welfare state was loosening the country's moral fibre, in his opinion; the continuing withdrawal from empire was an economic necessity, perhaps, but sad, almost a betrayal. Having a short time before accepted an army pension, and being a bachelor, he was free to go where he pleased.

Fern Park, a Georgian 'big house' on one hundred wooded acres, was an amputee, cut off from its erstwhile huge estate which, at the turn of the century, had passed into the ownership of numerous farmers. The house, formerly dominant in Fernboro, was for most of the year occupied only by a housekeeper and her handyman husband. Philip resided in a cottage adjacent to the main avenue.

From the top-storey windows of the big house he could see the verdant, jigsaw-patterned fields across the river. The pleasure he derived from this view declined with the development—or as he termed it, 'the disgraceful destruction'—of the countryside. Year after year, hedges and spinneys disappeared and then, to hasten the process, the ubiquitous chainsaw appeared, ravenously buzzing as it demolished stately trees. Frequently he saw radiating rainbows in the river: oil-slicks, evidence of pollution that had killed fish in the salmon-rich Fern on a number of occasions. The town, too, was changing.

Religion afforded him some solace. He liked to think that his parents had worshipped in St James's, and when entering the church he always paused in the porch which contained plaques commemorating parishioners killed in the Boer War and Great War. Fernboro's Protestants were clearly identified as a community within a community, fulfilling an unconscious need in Philip, one that the army had previously satisfied. The old ladies of the congregation remembered the splendidly uniformed British officers of their youth who adorned services in St James's, symbolising the unity of religion and empire. His father had been one of those officers. Philip lent a hand or, rather, was exhibited at harvest festivals, bazaars, flower shows, and only occasionally did he feel a touch of claustrophobia in this introverted environment of decaying gentility.

Gradually the old ladies and the old men joined a much larger congregation in the churchyard. Graves were submerged under briars and nettles, ivy webbed the headstones and the church fell into disrepair. Enrolments in the Protestant school plummeted and there was a real risk that it would close and force those parents who could not afford boarding school fees to send their children to the Catholic school instead. Issues like this became a worry for Philip and his co-religionists.

Then, with the growth in the country's economy and the advent of ecumenism, came changes. Fernboro's Protestant population, which for years had declined because of emigration and intermarriage with Catholics, slowly started to rise. Catholics could, without fear of eternal damnation, attend the funerals and weddings of their Protestant friends, and Protestants discovered that the Mass was not diabolical. The townspeople, both Catholic and Protestant, paid for the repair of St James's Church. Even the clock in the crenellated tower was restored to working order and volunteers cleared up the churchyard. There were those who growled at the changes, rather like animals roused from hibernation and evicted from cosy lairs, but Philip found no difficulty in combining tolerance with respect for tradition.

———————

Heinrich and Carmel treated Philip as one of the family, and their son, Eamonn, had from early childhood called him Uncle. The steady expansion of Heinrich's machine-component factory delighted Philip, although he might have regarded the factory as a blot on the landscape had it belonged to somebody else.

When he and Philip discussed the war, as they did quite frequently, Heinrich exercised a vigilant self-censorship. He had a deep respect for Philip, whom he regarded as the decent soldier personified, if slightly simplistic in his opinions. Simplistic or not, some of his comments reawakened questions in Heinrich. Like most people with a revived interest in religion, the reconverted, so to speak, Philip enjoyed talking about the subject, without, he emphasised, proselytising intent.

'Protestantism,' he said on one occasion, 'is synonymous with freedom. It expects a chap to think for himself. Which means that he won't accept too much nonsense from the damn fool politicians. Look at Europe. Communism has failed dismally to secure a grip in Britain, Scandinavia, the Netherlands, all traditionally Protestant. Whereas even in Western Europe, communism is strongest in Catholic countries like Italy and France. And it was a similar story with fascism, still is in Spain.'

'You are being selective,' Heinrich responded. 'For example, when it came to communism, what choice had a country such as Poland? And how do you explain Ireland? I doubt if you could find many supporters of Khrushchev here.'

Nevertheless, Heinrich wondered...

Around and around Munich's Karlsplatz walked a handsome young lieutenant who, to their chagrin, seemed oblivious of the glances of pretty girls. This was surprising because diversion should have been on his mind. He was on leave from Russia.

He left the Karlsplatz, hurried through several streets and into a church. Into a confessional he went. In the darkness, waiting for the priest to pull back the slide, he suppressed an urge to flee.

'My son, you were doing your duty,' droned the disembodied voice. 'For your penance reverently say three Lord's Prayers.'

He knelt before the altar but couldn't pray. He was incredulous at, felt cheated by, the paucity of the penance. Full of bitterness, yet with reluctance, he left the church.

He next entered a church shortly before his marriage.

Were Catholics, because of the dogmatic nature of their religion, more susceptible than others to authoritarianism?

Heinrich's parents had been devout Catholics, and so was Carmel, and she ensured that he accompanied her to Sunday Mass and received the sacraments. He desperately wanted to believe; he wished he were like St Augustine from whom 'all the darkness of uncertainty vanished away.'

Decanter of brandy within reach, Heinrich and Philip were tranquilly dozing when Carmel entered the room. She pulled a chair towards the fire.

'There's a film on television if you want to see it,' she said.

'Is it a Western?' asked Heinrich, who shared with Philip a fondness for the genre.

'No, I don't think so,' Carmel replied.

'Television—the opium of the people,' Philip muttered, half-asleep. 'Marx is outdated.'

Keeping her expression serious, Carmel faced Philip. 'You wouldn't want to quote Marx to Mr Donoghue. You'd spoil his Christmas.'

In moments of fantasy, Philip conjectured that he might have married someone like Carmel had he been younger when he arrived in Ireland; but at heart he knew he was engaging in wishful thinking. He had revered his mother, despite her practical desertion of him, and he had in consequence been inclined to idolise women, discovering only too late that many of them were averse to excessive reverence. Amused, he pretended to rise to Carmel's bait.

'The first thing that fellow will do will be to inspect the peacock on the lawn. I'm not really steward at all. That damned bird is!'

Mr Donoghue, an American, was reputed to be fabulously wealthy, and he had purchased what remained of Fern Park because his great-grandfather, great-grandmother, or some such personage—Philip could never unravel the genealogy—had come from Fernboro; or as Donoghue insisted, had been forced to emigrate by the rapaciousness of the Bournes. Fern Park had, for over two hundred years, been the seat of the landlord Bournes who, having dissipated their wealth, had sunk into oblivion. A crumbling ornate vault in St James's churchyard was now their only dwelling in Fernboro. Donoghue, according to Philip, was a cold fish, but he paid a good salary and his sojourns in Fernboro were infrequent.

Carmel's laughter was interrupted by a knock on the hall door. She left the room.

'Who was that?' Heinrich asked when she returned.

'A girl from the camp up the road,' said Carmel, resuming her seat.

Eamonn Obermeyer, sauntering along the avenue to his home, looked into a face that, for an instant, emerged from the twilight. Wordlessly the girl passed by, a trim figure in a pale frock, plastic bag in one hand. He looked round and so did she. He turned away and she did the same.

———————

'I won't!'

'You will!'

'Why do I always have to be one of them?'

"Cause your daddy's one.'

'It's not fair.'

'It is!'

Eamonn had much preferred to play Cowboys and Indians because he was often allowed to be a cowboy. Sometimes he was even in the cavalry. But when they played soldiers he was a Jerry and he was called a Hun and a Kraut and he hated being a Kraut because when he was on holidays in Bavaria he had eaten sauerkraut and it had made him sick. And he was expected to say stupid things like *Achtung* and Britisher and Englander and Yankie. The biggest and strongest boys and the fastest runners were British and American. Whoever was left was a Jerry. Nuala Corkery, a girl, was a Jerry. But the worst thing was that the Jerries never won. Everybody knew that because it was in the films and comics.

Then he overheard his father and Uncle Philip talking about Rommel and Uncle Philip said he had fought against him in the desert and he was a great general. After that he didn't mind being a Jerry provided he was Rommel.

Tata...tata...tat. Machine guns blazing the tank roared down the avenue between the whizzing trees of an oasis. A pull of a string and it veered right. Out of the oasis and into the garden it clanked, desert sand whirling from its tracks, scattering British from its path. Tata...tat. And the British general, Senan Murphy, was dead, but he didn't lie down. Senan always got mad when he was killed.

Besides, he was jealous of the tank that Eamonn and his father had made from pram wheels and tubular steel and wood. Usually it was powered by Nuala. She was a big girl of twelve and well able to shove.

A film about Rommel was shown in the cinema and they all went to see it, and Senan said it wasn't fair that Eamonn was always Rommel. Then, within a few weeks, all but Eamonn got fed up with Rommel and all the best boys were British and American again and they always won.

When he was ten Eamonn spent a whole month in Germany and flew home on his own. His parents had returned earlier. He could speak lots of German, and did so, but his friends said he was showing off and told him to shut up. But shortly afterwards their attitudes towards him changed: they had watched a television documentary containing newsreels from the 1930s.

He too was impressed by the documentary which his mother, saying it could do him no harm, had allowed him to see despite his father's objections. The pictures mesmerised him: rows and rows of soldiers, huge flags with the strange cross, lights shining up to the sky, people, thousands of people, raising their arms up to the man with the little moustache, the sound of everyone shouting together, music that made you want to leap from your chair, and the hoarse voice of the man with the moustache.

They talked about it for days. Senan Murphy said what he liked best were all the boys in uniform, singing, and they had their own banners and they all marched in step. Nuala said she had seen girls marching but no one else could remember seeing them.

His pals, Eamonn noticed proudly, became attentive to his father, according him almost as much respect as they gave to Esko. Esko was Cathal Corkery's dog, an elkhound, the only one in Fernboro, that made friends on its own terms. Eamonn guarded his privileged position, seeking his father's company at every opportunity, and conversing with him in German. But he was taken aback when his father said he wanted to be addressed in English when others were present. To do otherwise, his father said, was bad manners, like whispering in company. Eamonn didn't speak so much German after that.

And after a while the British and Americans resumed their victorious ways and Eamonn dismissed Nuala, his second-in-command. She was always giggling and she fraternised with the enemy: he found her behind a bush kissing an American.

Eamonn, lying on the bed, hands behind his head, grinned at the recollection, and thought of how everyone had been amazed when Nuala entered a convent. His mother, looking wise, had said the wild ones often made the best nuns. He believed that he understood Nuala's decision; since he had grown up and had started reading those books he had conceived a disgust for the world. He might even go into a monastery. Or he might change his name.

He raised himself and rested his back against the pillow and from across the room a book, yellow capitals on its spine, beckoned to him. He got off the bed, as he did so catching a satisfying glimpse of himself in the dressing-table mirror. He was nearly as tall as his father, whose well-cut features he had inherited; he had his mother's colouring except for his eyes: sky-blue they were, the same colour as his Grandmother Obermeyer's. So his father said.

Holding the book he flopped back on to the bed, enjoying the trampoline-effect of the well-sprung mattress. Schoolbooks lay undisturbed on a chair beside the bed. He reasoned that it was only October and the Leaving Certificate examination was far in the future, in June. He opened the book where it was marked by a dog-ear.

Eamonn had transferred to the adult section of the library when he was thirteen and, taste whetted by the television documentary that had never left his mind, devoured illustrated books on the Nazi period, entering an exciting, yet ordered world that made his own life appear dull.

His father told him not to leave the books lying around the place and added something about having enough worries without having to look at them. His mother looked at the pictures and said wasn't it all a terrible waste of energy.

He graduated to military history, and Heinz Guderian, master of the *Blitzkrieg*, replaced Rommel as his favourite general. At this stage Eamonn envisaged blood flowing through his veins in parallel streams, German and Irish, and he liked to imagine that the German stream was the broader. He was delighted when reference was made to his German ancestry.

'Obermeyer, you explain this formula. The Germans are good at this sort of thing,' Brother Mulhare used to say in the school science laboratory. Of course there was a price to pay; he spent a lot of time studying formulae.

Then there was Philip—Eamonn had dropped the 'uncle'—who with little prompting aired his views on military matters and addressed him as 'my dear chap' and 'old man'. Philip said that in his professional opinion the Germans were splendid soldiers.

Philip wasn't so forthcoming lately. 'Your father would not care to hear me talking to you about those unfortunate occurrences,' he said.

Unfortunate occurrences. What an euphemism! thought Eamonn, shifting on the bed as if to ease a feeling of contempt. A word in the book caught his eye: Resettlement. That was another euphemism. So was final solution.

Up to a year ago—or was it longer?—he had been such a credulous fool—until he borrowed from the library a book whose jacket showed a swastika on a plinth of skulls. Around the same time he had punched Senan Murphy for jestingly calling him a Hun, a sobriquet that Senan had frequently applied to him before without any unpleasant consequences.

Allowing the book to fall on to his stomach, he closed his eyes and his head sank into the pillow. He had read about atrocities so depraved and so extensive in scale that they blurred the mind like a soporific, lulling you into a surrealistic world so that after a while you were no longer shocked or even surprised by what you read. The same thing might have happened to the perpetrators of the atrocities, he surmised. Thank God he knew where his father had been during the war.

Chapter 3

Mary McCarthy had an indistinct conception of the picture she presented to others. Apart from a small looking-glass in her parents' caravan, her world was practically mirrorless. Reflections of herself glimpsed in shop windows, in pools of water, on shiny surfaces, pleased her. She was neat and well proportioned, with shoulder-length black hair and eyes that were dark-brown, yet translucent. Her nose was slightly tip-tilted, and had the effect of making her look younger than her age. Her teeth she kept clean with salt because she seldom had toothpaste.

After emerging from the avenue, Mary stopped to open the plastic bag: full packets of tea and sugar, a large loaf, a pound of butter, a pot of marmalade. She'd been right: the people in the house in the trees were real quality. Were they Protestants, she wondered.

The woman of the house left the door ajar as she was putting things into the plastic bag. Mary stood on the stone steps in the flow of warm air from the hall, inhaling the delicate fragrance of food. Leaves rustled in the evening breeze that ruffled her flimsy frock and chilled her sandal-clad, stockingless feet. Into the hall she peered, at the crimson carpet, the velvety wallpaper, the mahogany hallstand, the crystal chandelier.

'Call back in a few days and I'll have a few clothes gathered for you,'

24

said the woman, handing Mary the plastic bag.

'The blessings of God and his Holy Mother on you,' intoned Mary, like a child reciting esoteric verse. Her mother said you should always show you were grateful; at least you should pretend you were. And if you were given something, you should try and get a bit more. But that wasn't necessary in this case because the woman had offered clothes without being asked. Her mother also said it was better to deal with the real quality. They didn't shout or threaten you.

Not like some of the people in the houses near the camp, houses to which Mary had called earlier in the evening. After a weekend of plenty, the McCarthys' resources were scarce. Tom had a few pounds, but he said he needed the money for petrol and porter.

During the day, Sheila and Tom Junior and Davy had been dispatched by Maggie on a mendicant expedition, but they returned with very little, just two pints of milk and a packet of biscuits. These they had stolen from a shop, but Maggie asked no questions. Instead she upbraided them on their meagre pickings, until the sight of Davy clutching the biscuits—they were chocolate-covered—mellowed her annoyance and disappointment.

'You'll have to go,' she said, turning to Mary. 'Whatever about anything else, get a bit of tae and sugar.'

Begging was a way of life for Mary from the time she was a babe in arms. Her earliest memories were of standing close to her mother at street corners, in a forest of legs, nyloned and trousered and bare. Now and then faces appeared in the forest, faces at her own level, faces of children, timid and suspicious and curious and smiling and talking faces. The talking faces, the ones she liked best, were usually reafforested rapidly, yanked out of sight amid admonitions from on high. Other words and sounds came from on high: her mother chanting, 'A few coppers, Mam', 'A few coppers, Sir'; coins clinking in her mother's bowl. Occasionally, as though tree-branches were brushing her with leaves, her hair was patted and voices said, 'Isn't she a lovely little girl'; 'She's a dote'; 'Oh, she's pretty'; and the bowl would clink, a chain of clinks. And she would be happy because she knew the clinks made her mother happy.

Begging from door to door one rainy day, she pulled a corner of her mother's shawl over her head and shoulders, but her mother whisked the shawl away. She was soaked, but the more bedraggled she became the more was given them at each door.

Mary had come to expect taunts and insults, and she had learned to give as good as she got, but there were incidents she couldn't anticipate. A few years before she rang a doorbell which was answered by a boy not much older than she was. He grabbed her and pressed against her. He sniffed. 'All knackers stink, but I'd smell you any time,' he sneered. She was sure that he wouldn't belittle a girl of the settled community like that. She covertly watched them, these girls, her contemporaries, all dressed alike in school uniforms, carrying books, laughing and chattering together. An odd one might utter a faint greeting, but mostly they ignored her, treated her as if she were invisible.

Mary began her quest for tea and sugar, irritably thinking of how she would like to clout Sheila for her failure to acquire the commodities. 'That little bitch,' she muttered, substituting verbal vehemence for physical retribution.

Anxious for a quick end to the quest, Mary pressed the doorbell of the house nearest the camp. As the peals faded, a figure was outlined in the glass panels of the door and it was opened by a woman with a cat at her feet. When she saw Mary the woman snatched up the cat. The door slammed.

On Mary walked, into a cul-de-sac lined with bungalows. She knocked on a door. A slight movement in a curtain. She knocked again. The next three doors also remained closed and Mary suspected that people were forewarned of her approach. She skipped several houses, then approached one with a lace-curtained bay-window through which she could see a bluish haze. She edged closer to the window, but she couldn't distinguish the television screen. The television laughed tinnily, emptily.

Mary walked on. 'Did you not see the sign?' a swanky-looking woman demanded from her doorway, her voice rising over the yaps of a Jack Russell terrier. 'Get away or I'll let the dog out.'

Mary retraced her steps and deliberately left the gate open. 'Beware of Dog' said the sign on the gate, but she couldn't read it. She couldn't read anything. Ned, her brother, had a watch, but only for show. He couldn't tell the time. Mary had never met a traveller who could read. They put their mark, usually an X, on the bottom of forms.

Nuns had instructed her for First Holy Communion and for Confirmation, and that was the only schooling she had got. Yet she liked books, ones with pictures, comics. Even her parents enjoyed comics because they could make out the stories from the pictures.

A mental picture of the boy she had met on the avenue to the house in the trees absorbed and vaguely agitated Mary on her way back to the camp. She heard someone call her name. Mikey Driscoll, in a half-trot, was coming towards her. The Driscolls had arrived in the camp on the previous day and almost immediately Mikey had started gadding around her, smiling like an eejit when she spoke to him, and with a face like a hungry greyhound when she ignored him. She had enjoyed it at first but now wished that he would go away and find someone his own age. He was twenty-two at least and she didn't want her father to get any stupid ideas. The previous night she had overheard her father praising Mikey and saying that he would be a good match. Mikey had a big van and dealt in carpets and furniture.

Lying in a tent warmed by the breath of sleeping children, Mary strove to stay awake so that she could continue to think about the boy on the avenue. When sleep claimed her, she dreamed, and he was in the dreams. Impossible dreams.

Chapter 4

Helen Moran wondered if she should suggest a prayer to start the meeting; then compromising, she mentally recited a Hail Mary. Despite the frosty weather it was warm, almost too warm, in the Murphys' sitting-room. She leaned back, extended her right arm, and tentatively touched the radiator behind her chair. She quickly withdrew her hand. She unbuttoned her coat and loosened her scarf, practical garments of dark green and pale brown, respectively. Of slight build, she wore no make-up, and her greying hair was cut short. Her expression was placid, her features fine but clearly etched.

People leaned against the walls and perched two to a chair. Conversations mingled, but the men standing just inside the door —Helen recognised them as being from the Council estate—said little, as if they were unsure of their welcome.

A bookcase enshrining mint volumes of *Encyclopaedia Britannica* was built into an alcove beside the fireplace and formed a backdrop for Joe Murphy, who sat behind a paper-strewn coffee table, facing the door, in navy pinstripe suit, light-blue shirt, and wine tie. In a matching alcove on the other side of the fireplace was a cabinet with a display of silver and Irish crystal that drew envious looks from the ladies. On top of the cabinet was a framed photograph of the youngest Murphy child, a girl. Helen smiled wistfully at the photograph, regretting that colour film was rare when her children were babies. Joe straightened the knot of his tie, rose from his chair, and coughed lightly. Cigarette-smoke was fogging the atmosphere. Conversations petered out as eyes locked on him and he began to speak.

'Ladies and gentlemen, I want to thank you for coming here tonight. During the past few weeks I have talked to many of you and I think we all agree that something will have to be done about this problem. I am as tolerant as anyone and I didn't mind when there were only one or two families up there, but it has reached the stage where we are nearly overrun with these people, not to mention their dogs and horses. We have put up with this situation for the best part of two months and some are suffering worse than others. Take Mrs Moran, for instance; maybe she'd tell you herself? She's even embarrassed to look out her windows.'

Murmurs of sympathy rippled through the room. Mrs Moran was popular, a good neighbour, Auntie Helen to many children.

Helen blushed. 'I'm no good at public speaking,' she said falteringly. 'You continue, Mr Murphy.'

Joe resumed. 'There are ladies present, so I will not be explicit, but there's a hedge a short distance from Mrs Moran's house and…'

Pictures of squatting figures were projected on Helen's mind. They were savages, just like beasts, she thought. Before the weather turned cold the stench was terrible and she had to close windows against the flies. Noise from the camp kept her awake at night and one or other of them was always knocking on the door. Giving them anything was a waste of time; clothes were left to rot on the side of the road. They said they wanted to settle down but they weren't fit to be in houses. She had read reports about how they had wrecked houses they had been given. They had even stabled animals in houses while they themselves camped outside. Not that they were kind to animals. On several occasions she'd seen them unmercifully lashing ponies and donkeys.

Helen believed all itinerants were alike, and she accepted Joe Murphy's assertion that their presence in an area lowered property values. After her husband had died suddenly, leaving her an electrical appliance shop in Fernboro, she had sold the business and bought a house on River Road, and this was her chief, practically her sole asset. With quiet determination, and unshakable religious convictions, she struggled to rear her children on a widow's pension. The children had won university scholarships: her daughter, who was twenty-four, was now a secondary schoolteacher in Dublin, while her son, two years younger, an engineer, was doing a term of voluntary service in Africa, much to his mother's approval.

'... and we would be failing in our duty as citizens and Christians if we ignored the plight of Mrs Moran and other vulnerable members of our community.' Heads nodded in agreement.

Joe continued. 'We all know what happens when itinerants move into an area. Apart from everything else, they bring dirt around a place and create a health hazard. In this context I am thinking particularly of our children; practically everyone here has young children. And as for property; itinerants have no respect for other people's property.'

'You'd want to pin everything down with a six-inch nail,' interjected a shrill female voice, which was followed by other voices castigating the sins of itinerants. 'There's rats up in the camp as big as cats,' someone could be heard remarking above the general babble.

Joe felt it was time to deliver what he regarded as the crucial portion of his address; magnanimity was called for, an appeal to common interests. Statesmanship would be the term used in a wider arena. He tapped his Parker ball-point on the table for silence. 'Now I know that some of us have had our differences,' he said solemnly. He paused, looked towards the men near the door before proceeding. 'Mistakes were made by all of us, but I, for my part, am prepared to let bygones be bygones. I would appeal for an united front on this issue. If we are to solve this problem we must stand together.'

Bill Sullivan, one of the men near the door, knew that Murphy's remarks were directed mainly towards him. There Murphy stood, at the top of the room, cheeks the same colour as his tie, cuff-links glistening as he gesticulated, a stocky figure thatched with grey-brown, back-combed hair. Like a fighting cock, thought Bill. Cock Murphy. That's what the lads in Tuohy Place called him. Still, you had to admit that Murphy was talking sense for a change. Yesterday morning Bill was astonished to receive in the post a typed invitation to a meeting in Murphy's house. It was his first invitation to a house across the Berlin Wall.

In recent years the town of Fernboro had oozed over much of the surrounding countryside, including River Road. Farmers whose forefathers had complained of lack of land and rack-rents cheerfully pocketed inflated sums for sites, while many of the town's streets, lined with crumbling buildings and rubble-strewn wastelands, looked like gap-toothed mouths. River View Drive, a leafy cul-de-sac (mainly flowering cherries) containing eighteen detached and individual bungalows, became one of Fernboro's most desirable addresses.

The idyllic existence of Joe Murphy and his neighbours in River View Drive changed on a bright April morning four years before, when earth-moving machinery began gobbling up soil in a nearby field. Within a year, workmen were slating the roofs of Tuohy Place. The cherry trees, even in full blossom, could do little to camouflage the ugly houses whose upper windows peeped into River View Drive. Tuohy Place, named in honour of a politician who had served forty years in public office, consisted of thirty Town Council houses crowded in six blocks around an oblong green.

Joe felt cheated: he and his neighbours had paid good money to live on River Road, unlike the people, many of them riff-raff, who'd do nothing to help themselves, who were being brought into the area by the Council. Driving home one evening he saw a young woman pushing a pram out of Tuohy Place, cigarette hanging from her lips, child clinging to her coat. He shuddered.

He decided it was time to segregate River View Drive from Tuohy Place. He and his neighbours formally and successfully requested the Town Council to build a wall between the two neighbourhoods. Led by Bill Sullivan, the tenants of Tuohy Place angrily demanded that work should cease on what they called the Berlin Wall, a term eagerly seized by the newspapers which, to the annoyance of River View Drive people, blazed it in headlines.

Joe Murphy was used to, and indeed, courted publicity, but not publicity of this sort. It was all very well when his name and picture appeared in the local newspaper in connection with his business or with his membership of the rugby and golf clubs, or as a record of his attendance at an important function or dinner. But now he was being forced into a public slagging match with the crowd in Tuohy Place. In a carefully composed and, he thought, reasonable statement to the newspapers, he claimed that the people of River View Drive were trying only to preserve the 'residential character' of their area.

The statement fuelled the anger of Tuohy Place. Bill Sullivan issued a retaliatory statement accusing River View Drive residents of snobbery. *Do they want us to be caged like animals?* he wondered.

In his heart of hearts Bill conceded that some of the tenants of Tuohy Place weren't the type of people he'd have picked as neighbours if he'd had a choice. But the vast majority were like himself, hard-working, good-humoured people, who were in Council houses because they couldn't afford to build their own homes and whose only vice was a few pints, mostly at weekends, and an odd flutter. Not like the carry-on of the so-called nobs.

Bill gave credence to rumours about the golf club, which was patronised by many River View Drive people, rumours about late-night wife-swapping parties. They helped to assuage his feeling of inferiority. He also consoled himself by thinking of Ted Corkery who lived in River View Drive. Corkery was a contractor, but he had started off as a chippie. Bill, too, was a carpenter, the first of his family to acquire a trade.

Bill was secretly flattered by the invitation to Joe Murphy's bungalow. He entered the bungalow, the biggest in River View Drive, with apprehension; it was like entering enemy territory. Though the battle of the Berlin Wall had petered out two years previously, the wounds hadn't fully healed. About five feet tall, the wall represented a compromise that satisfied nobody. To the residents of River View Drive it was just a symbolic dividing line, not the real barrier they had demanded. To the tenants of Tuohy Place it was an insult, designed to keep them physically and socially in their place.

Joe droned on about community relations and Bill's mind wandered. He admired the elaborate cornices. He was almost sure that the carved fireplace was oak. This room is larger than any two in my house, he thought. Like all the houses in Tuohy Place, Bill's home was cramped, and would shortly be more so because another child was on the way; he already had two, a boy aged five and a girl of three. Not bad going, he mused, for a fellow of twenty-five.

'Mr Sullivan! Mr Sullivan!'

A nudge from his neighbour, Jim Walsh, restored Bill to the present. Joe Murphy, turned slightly sideways with his extended fingers just touching the coffee table, was focusing on Bill through the cigarette-smoke, as was everyone else; those on chairs had twisted round to view him.

The women, even the women of River View Drive, enjoyed the view. During the controversy over the Berlin Wall they had applied the epithet, 'common', to the tenants of Tuohy Place. Disconcertingly, Bill didn't fit into this category. He had a respectable appearance, and he was good-looking: body honed by manual work, regular features retaining an adolescent freshness. Tonight he was dressed up in his best clothes.

'Mr Sullivan, I was wondering whether you'd agree with my suggestion—I'll make it a proposal—that we should establish a special committee to combat the itinerant problem?' asked Joe Murphy. 'What I have in mind is a committee representing all the residents of River Road and I'm sure everyone here would want you to be a member of it.'

Bill seemed to ponder for a moment. He was, in fact, savouring the situation: Murphy had actually asked for his opinion! 'I think that is a very good idea, Mr Murphy,' he replied. 'I'll second your proposal.'

'Are all in favour of the proposal?' asked Joe, relieved. There was a chorus of assent and he declared the proposal formally adopted. Then began the process of electing people to the committee: River View Drive and Tuohy Place were allocated three representatives each. Joe Murphy and Bill Sullivan were unanimously chosen as chairman and vice-chairman, respectively, of what was to be officially known as River Road Residents' Association.

'Our next task is to decide precisely on what action we should take,' said Joe, seating himself again. 'Of course we all are aware of the purpose of any action we may decide upon: to get rid of the itinerants once and for all.'

'Mr Chairman.' A bespectacled, ascetic-looking man had risen from the crowd. Joe recognised Mr Fitzharris whom, frankly, he was surprised to see at the meeting. He was courteous but kept very much to himself. He was regarded as somewhat of an eccentric, absorbed in his own thoughts, unaware of the stares and giggles of children, who were fascinated by the bushy eyebrows that highlighted his total baldness.

'Where do you expect them to go?' he asked quietly, his pate white in the electric light.

Joe stood up. 'What exactly do you mean, Mr Fitzharris?' he parried.

'I mean, Mr Chairman, that the itinerants, like the rest of us, have to live somewhere. If you want them out of this area, which you obviously do, then surely you should suggest an alternative and suitable place of residence for them.'

The shrill female voice, heard earlier, intervened again and Joe was glad of the intervention. This time it was just short of a scream. 'The tinkers should be sent out to the country somewhere. They shouldn't be allowed next or near a town.'

'With all due respects, Mr Fitzharris,' said Joe, recovering his equanimity, 'I don't think that is our responsibility. It's a matter for the government and local authorities.'

Shouts of 'Hear, Hear' drowned Mr Fitzharris's voice and he resumed his seat.

The remainder of the meeting proceeded smoothly. Two decisions were made: all River Road householders would be requested to sign a petition calling for the removal of itinerants from the area; and the petition would be presented to the Town Council.

After the meeting, Joe Murphy shook hands with Bill Sullivan.

'You could be the very man I need,' said Joe. 'You're a carpenter, I believe?'

'Yes, that's right.'

'If you have a few minutes to spare, there's something I'd like you to have a look at.'

In bed that night his wife complained of whiskey on Bill's breath.

Helen Moran's two-storeyed house stood alone, between River View Drive and the itinerant camp. On her way home from the meeting she thanked God for giving her caring neighbours. Her other neighbours were quiet tonight. Only the glow of their camp-fires, clear in the frosty air, disclosed their presence.

When he arrived home, Noel Fitzharris raked the fire and put on more coal. He plugged in the kettle and then instinctively turned towards the crammed bookshelves. But he wasn't in the mood for reading, at least not until after he'd had a cup of tea. He wished that he were still living in the country, amidst the quiet fields, away from River View Drive.

It wasn't an incapacity for work that had brought about Noel's retirement from farming: he'd retired because of his distaste for what he regarded as the growing hypocrisy of the agricultural community. Shortly after expressing this view openly, he was relieved of his post as Honorary Secretary of Fernboro Farmers' Alliance. He had originally been pressurised into accepting the secretaryship because of his reputation as 'a great man for the reading and writing'; he was a bibliophile and an acknowledged local historian.

Farmers, Noel decided, had become beggars who persisted in abusing their benefactors. The benefactors were the government and the workers who paid income tax. Yet, paradoxically, farmers insisted on being treated as a superior class. Granted, there was a time when farmers had every reason to be proud, when they'd had a sturdy stand-on-your-own-feet attitude. But now, Noel concluded, that pride was a sham.

Anyway, he now knew that he should never have been a farmer. The farm should have gone to his sister—he had no brothers—who had loved the land. His father had removed him from school, protesting, at the age of fifteen. His sister went to work as a typist in London and had recently died there.

Noel was a bachelor, not from preference, but because he was certain that no girl would form a union with someone of his unprepossessing appearance. He was one of Ireland's innumerable, apparently asexual celibates. Two years before, he had moved to River View Drive. The move, a distance of three miles, was more traumatic than he had anticipated. He was the last of a long line of Fitzharrises and he was choking with loneliness, an exile's loneliness, as he closed the farm-house door for the final time. He handed the heavy old-fashioned key to Peter Ahern, who had purchased the farm. Peter didn't really need the key, for within a fortnight he had demolished the house. Destroyed, too, were the garden, the beeches, and most of the stone sheds.

Since his retirement, Noel had fulfilled his expectation of being able to devote more attention to his books and to history research, but he hadn't, as he had hoped, acquired new friends. He found it difficult to relate to the residents of River View Drive, and, he sensed, vice versa. His sister used to tell him that in England people often didn't know their neighbours but he had found it difficult to believe. Now he was beginning to understand that phenomenon. He regarded himself as a liberal, a member of the liberal middle-class that was changing Ireland. River View Drive was a middle-class estate but any liberalism that existed there was based on selfishness, not on idealism. To his intense dismay, it had revealed its true nature on the itinerant issue.

One Sunday morning ten years previously Noel had stopped abruptly in the act of knotting his tie. He stared into the mirror on the wardrobe door and admitted: I've lost my religion. He was frightened at first, a man cast without a lifebelt on the sea; then he laughed derisively. You coward, he chastised himself, it has taken you until now to admit something that you've known for a long, long time. His mother had warned that he would read himself out of his religion. She had been correct. He completed the knot on his tie. And he went to Mass. Though he had abandoned the sacraments, he still attended Mass every Sunday and sometimes on weekdays: it was an outing with the prospect of company. He was like a theatre-goer who is more interested in the audience than in the play.

Noel had lost his belief in Roman Catholicism, whose tenets and history he couldn't reconcile with the teachings of Christ. Catholicism was in his view a formula which had the effect of lessening one's responsibility for one's own actions; and in Ireland, at least, it seemed to be preoccupied with temporalities in the guise of spiritualities. Had he been asked about his present beliefs, Noel would probably have replied that he was a Christian, a Christian anxious to give tangible assistance to his neighbour. In his experience, the opportunities for doing so were remarkably rare. Donating to charity was all very well, but it was just balm to the conscience, duty performed at a distance. No doubt there were needy people in and around Fernboro, but how did one get to know them? How could one help without patronising them?

He was still anxiously pondering these questions when he fell asleep that night.

Chapter 5

'We have visitors,' said Carmel. 'Joe Murphy and another man.'

'What can they want?' muttered Heinrich. After wiping his hands on a rag, he left the garden shed where he had been cleaning and oiling the lawnmower in preparation for its hibernation. It was the last Saturday in October, a muggy day without a hint of autumnal charm. He struggled out of his wellingtons, rejected the idea of donning slippers, put on shoes instead, and, accompanied by Carmel, went through the hallway and into what they called the big room, in effect the drawing room.

Joe Murphy greeted Heinrich, disparaged the weather, and introduced Bill Sullivan.

'You'll have a cup of tea or coffee?' said Carmel.

'No, thank you very much,' Joe replied. 'I'm afraid we haven't the time.' He briskly opened a plastic folder and extracted a foolscap sheet. 'We are hoping you will sign this,' he said, holding up the sheet. 'We have already called on a lot of people and we've had a nearly one hundred per cent response.'

Heinrich's immediate reaction was one of relief that Joe for once wasn't touting for business. He insured his car through Joe, who was a broker as well as being an auctioneer and agent for a building society.

'I know they can be a nuisance,' Carmel was saying. 'But you have to have some sympathy for them, particularly the children. It can't be easy for them in weather like this.'

'That's the kind of life they want,' Joe retorted. 'They haven't the same values or outlook as the rest of us. They want everything for nothing. When did you ever see one of them doing an honest day's work? They lash all their money on drink.'

'But surely there is genuine poverty among them?'

'They've only themselves to blame.'

Though she wouldn't openly acknowledge it, Carmel felt there was something in what Joe was saying: itinerants seemed to her to be their own worst enemies, creating ill-feeling through their drunkenness and quarrels. She believed they were schooled in deviousness, so she never fully trusted them, but neither did she especially dislike them.

'Parasites, that's what they are,' Joe exclaimed.

Heinrich, memory alerted, felt a gnawing unease. 'You are using strong terms, Joe,' he said quietly.

'I'm speaking the truth.'

'Do you know what the itinerants do?' The question shot from Bill Sullivan. 'I'll tell you. Every week they travel around in new vans from dole office to dole office and they're paid at each one. They get away with it because they sign with an X. And they go out robbing and selling scrap and carpets and the women and children go begging. They're better off than us. No one should give them anything.'

Bill's blue eyes were fixed fervently on Heinrich. Again Heinrich's memory stirred.

'They're not all the same,' said Carmel. 'A girl from the camp often calls here and I don't believe she'd harm a fly.'

'They're all like that,' Joe said. 'Cunning.' Why the hell, he asked himself, can't they sign the petition and stop beating round the bush? He uncrossed his legs, shifted in his chair, and the folder fell from his knees on to the floor. He grabbed it and continued. 'Those do-gooders who are always shedding tears over itinerants wouldn't be long changing their tune if they had to live near them. Let me ask you a question, Mrs Obermeyer: would you approve of your son marrying a tinker?'

'I...it would depend on the circumstances, I suppose,' replied Carmel, flustered.

Joe smiled condescendingly. Scenting victory, he turned to Heinrich. 'Would you employ one of them in your factory?'

'Whom I would employ or would not employ is a matter I prefer not to discuss,' Heinrich said coldly. That, he noted with grim satisfaction, wiped the damn smirk off Murphy's face. That would teach him to be impertinent to Carmel. Nevertheless, Heinrich was fully aware that he had side-stepped the question.

'The rain seems to be getting heavier,' interjected Carmel.

'Yes, it's really coming down now,' agreed Bill..

'I hope it doesn't muck up the ground too much; we have a rugby match tomorrow,' said Joe, quickly regaining his sang-froid.

'Are you still playing the game?' asked Heinrich politely.

'Good God, no!' Joe laughed and patted his paunch, which even the skilful cut of his fur-collared, sheepskin car-coat could not disguise. 'But I'm hoping that Bill here will soon line out for us. We could do with strong lads like him.'

He stood up and produced a pen from inside his coat. 'Well, if you'll sign this we'll be on our way,' he said, smoothing the foolscap sheet on top of the folder.

'Joe, I'm sure you can appreciate that Carmel and I need some time to think about this.'

The play had again departed from the script. Joe fiddled with his pen. Then, managing to keep his voice steady, he said, 'That's fair enough, Heinrich. I have no doubt that you'll come around to our point of view. We'll call again.'

Back in the shed, Heinrich switched on the light. The day had darkened and rain rattled on the galvanised roof. After the encounter with Joe Murphy, he had come immediately to resume his overhaul of the lawnmower and inspect and clean garden tools. But he just sat on an upturned wooden box under the naked light-bulb, looking towards the window. The outside darkness transformed the window into a mirror, a mirror cracked by raindrops, reflecting a pensive, greying figure, crinkled skin around the eyes, jowls shadowed.

Heinrich saw his image, not in the window-mirror, but in his memory: a tanned youth in open-necked shirt and *lederhosen*.

'Heinrich, you are very innocent.'

His best friend, Ernst Hinterberger, leaned against a tree, leaf-filtered sunlight dappling his bare torso, wave of blonde hair on his forehead, styled in imitation of his hero.

'But, Ernst, I am thinking of the ones we know, people we have known all our lives.'

Ernst spat out a blade of grass he'd been chewing. 'Yes, but look at how well-off they all are,' he said. 'Look at the shops and houses they own in town. Where do you think they got the money? They're like leeches, fattening on our blood.'

'Ah, that's a bit of an exaggeration.'

'Are you doubting Adolf Hitler? He's Head of State, not some corner-boy, and if you don't believe him you won't believe anyone. Hasn't he stuck to his word about bringing down unemployment? Didn't he say he would get back the Rhineland and hasn't he done so? It stands to reason that what he says about them is correct!'

'But the ones around here; they are pleasant people.'

Smiling broadly, Ernst punched his companion lightly on the shoulder. 'You cannot deceive me with your talk about pleasant people. I know who's on your mind!'

Heinrich turned his face into the soft, cooling breeze.

'Adela Ornstein is a fine piece of skirt. But that's all she is,' Ernst continued.

Heinrich suppressed the urge to strike his friend. A display of anger would be too revealing.

'She's like the rest of them,' Ernst said. 'They have different standards from us. Be realistic, Heinrich. Think of the consequences of being serious about her. Think of what your family would say.'

Heinrich went home that night with a copy of *Der Stürmer* that had been loaned to him by Ernst. Heinrich's father, on seeing the paper, said: 'I am surprised and disappointed to observe you with that publication. Please keep it out of this house.' His tone was quiet and cutting, a sure indication of displeasure.

Der Stürmer gained a regular and eager subscriber in Heinrich, who smuggled it to his bedroom where, behind a locked door, and shamefaced at first, he dwelt on its lascivious, illustrated stories about the seduction of innocent Aryan girls by their evil Jewish employers.

The locked door wasn't really necessary because he knew that his parents, believing he was immersed in textbooks, would respect his plea to be left undisturbed. Still, it was safer to take precautions.

His estimation of the paper rose and his shame seemed needless when he discovered that it was published by a schoolteacher from Nuremberg. Many of his own teachers, men whom he respected, were ardent National Socialists, as indeed were most of his schoolmates. He thought of Ernst. Ernst was no *dummkopf*. He was always at or near top of the class.

Heinrich assured himself that he didn't take the stories in *Der Stürmer* seriously, that, unlike the average reader, he was intelligent enough to discern their satirical quality. But the stories, together with the prevailing ethos, insidiously polluted his perceptions. Really, he thought, they are at least partly responsible for their own predicament.

But not all Jews. Not Adela Ornstein.

———————

'Dad!' Eamonn, rain glistening on his face and hair, bounded into the shed. He stopped short when he saw his father. 'Are you OK?' he asked.

'Of course. I am fine.'

'Well, you look a bit...a bit downhearted.'

The realisation struck Heinrich that Eamonn was now around the same age as he and Ernst had been on that summer's day in Bavaria, and he experienced a surge of protective feeling towards his son.

'Mother says you're to come in. Lunch is ready.' Eamonn, appetite keen, departed.

———————

'Wouldn't you think a person in his position would have a bigger car?' said Joe Murphy. Heinrich's modest Ford saloon was parked in front of the Obermeyer house.

'This is a grand job,' said Bill Sullivan.

'I bought it only a month ago—it cost me a nice few thousand.' Joe guided the Audi 100 down the avenue, soothed by the purr of the engine which could just be heard through the rain and the swish of the windscreen wipers.

'Do you think they'll sign?' Bill asked.

'Oh, she'd sign but you wouldn't know with him. Did you see the way he reacted? Arrogant, like a fecking Nazi. We'll bring Helen Moran with us the next time; she'll help to persuade them.'

'Is Mrs Obermeyer from around here?'

'Yes. Do you know Peter Ahern? He's her brother.'

The Aherns weren't in the same league as the Thompsons, Joe reflected. The Thompsons were large farmers; among the largest around Fernboro, and Sandra was one of them. His marriage to her, or to be precise, the money she brought, was the lucky break he had needed. That and the sum the bank had paid him for the old house, a large sum because the house was in the Town Square, a prime location that the bank coveted for new offices. Though it had been in the Murphy family for generations, Joe was glad to sell the property. It had humiliating memories for him.

Memories of his father behind the counter, clinging to it. Of his mother despairingly trying to keep the auctioneering business going. Men who had rocked Joe on their knees and who had given him pennies and threepences and sixpences, and sometimes even half-crowns, no longer came in. Instead there were men and women all talking in a horrible flat way, calling him Joey and his father Joe. And the talking became shouting and the shouting always led to fighting (so it seemed in Joe's recollection) and the fighting was bloody. Then came the gardai. His father, tottering on the beer-soaked floor that was strewn with smashed glasses and broken stools, blinking and smiling imbecilically and grimacing as he was berated by the sergeant.

Joe Murphy is stuck-up,

But he comes from a tinkers' pub...

Children, mostly ragamuffins from the lanes, pranced behind Joe, taunting him, and there were adults who enjoyed the scene: a proud Fernboro family was hitting rock-bottom and the thud was thrilling.

Murphys had been part of the town's business life for almost a century, and a grand-uncle of Joe had represented the area in the British parliament. Traditionally, a Murphy helped carry the canopy over the Blessed Eucharist in processions—an honour confined to the elite—and the family paid a rent for an inviolable pew in St Bridget's Church.

Joe's father lost both privileges: he was banned from canopy-carrying after he wobbled against the parish priest, and he neglected to pay or was unable to afford the rent for the pew.

He died in 1942. The embossed inscription on the pub windows announcing *Select Lounge* and *Finest Wines and Spirits* was like an epitaph on a sarcophagus. The pub, licence sold a year previously, was closed.

There remained an auctioneer's certificate in the name of Joe's mother. Despite her misgivings—he was only seventeen—Joe went into business, cycling through the town and countryside canvassing for clients. Seven years later he married Sandra Thompson. Their sons were aged twenty-two and seventeen, and their daughter was nine. The eldest son, a trainee accountant, was shortly to join the family firm. Five people, including Joe, were now employed in the business which had its offices in High Street, in a premises that had been purchased with part of the proceeds from the sale of the old house to the bank. The sign over the offices always cheered Joe. *Murphy and Son* it proclaimed in large plastic lettering. The same as the sign over the old pub.

'Thanks for dropping me home,' said Bill Sullivan, alighting from the Audi.

'You're welcome. We've done a good morning's work—apart from the German.'

Joe drove away. He acknowledged the salutes and nods of several Tuohy Place people. They're not such a bad crowd around here after all, he thought.

———————

In the afternoon the rain stopped and Heinrich went walking in an effort to dispel the restlessness that had plagued him since his meeting with Murphy and Sullivan. He and Carmel strolled towards the town, then turned right into a side road, the Loop, a popular perambulation, that circled River Road for a distance of about two miles. For half a mile or so their arm-in-arm progress was silent, save for the crackle of their rubber-soled shoes on leaves in the lee of hedges.

'I must taste one of those,' said Carmel, detaching herself from Heinrich. She picked a purple sloe and popped it into her mouth. 'They're not as sweet as they should be after the frost. Do you want one?'

'No, they are too bitter for my taste.'

'Just like yourself.'

Carmel stepped away from the blackthorn bush and began to hurry along the road. 'What do you mean?' called Heinrich, breaking into a trot to catch up with her.

'I might as well be talking to myself for all the company you've been,' she said. 'You're brooding all day: it's as bad as the time when you used to read those German books.'

Heinrich thought of his now dusty volumes of philosophy and history and religion, inherited from his father. Many were scorched and scarred, as they had been salvaged from bomb rubble. They were books in which Heinrich had sought expiation. On his shelves, too, was a copy of *Mein Kampf*, a toxic weed amidst flowers, a recipe for damnation.

'Carmel, slow down. I know that I haven't been the best of company. Murphy and that other fellow soured my good humour.'

'Yes, that's another thing. I wasn't going to say anything, but now that you've brought it up yourself: why did you have to be so rude to Joe Murphy?' Carmel halted abruptly and faced Heinrich. 'And there's something else: you never seem to talk seriously to Eamonn. I have to do all the worrying about him. He's doing his Leaving Cert next year, but as far as I can see, he's reading library books when he should be studying.'

'What kind of books?'

'About things that happened during the war. The photographs in some of them would frighten anyone.'

Heinrich gazed at trees in the field behind Carmel.

'Are you listening to me at all?'

'Of course I am.' Heinrich caught Carmel's arm and tucked it under his own. They resumed walking.

She said, 'You haven't brought Eamonn to Bavaria for ages and I never hear the two of you talking together in German now. You should help him to put those books he's reading into context. You shouldn't brush off his questions.'

'I do not.'

'You do, particularly if they're about the war. I've often noticed it. Philip Shaw tells him more than you do.'

Not for the first time, Heinrich was sharply aware of his wife's perspicacity. 'I shall have a talk with Eamonn,' he promised.

Mollified, Carmel directed his attention to a holly bush, the berries and satiny leaves of which freshened a russet beech hedgerow. 'I must remember to get a bit of that for Christmas,' she said, 'if the birds haven't eaten all the berries by then.'

They left the Loop where it rejoined River Road and turned westwards towards home, passing between horses and donkeys and goats tethered on the grass margins. Smoke, blue against the grey of the sky, signalled the itinerant camp which, beyond a bend in the road, unfolded in a line of caravans, big and small, plain and elaborate, some with open doors, some with delf-laden tables just outside the doors, some fronted by aluminium milk-churns containing water, nearly all umbilically corded to gas cylinders. There were also a few horse-drawn caravans.

Heinrich and Carmel were anxious not to display unseemly curiosity and in unspoken agreement quickened their pace. It was as if they had stumbled upon a private gathering.

'Hello, mam. Hello, sir. A bad day.'

'Oh hello, Mary,' said Carmel, stopping because she didn't want to seem brusque. 'Yes, it is bad. It must be terrible for you with all that mud around the place.'

'We have to get used to it.'

Carmel addressed Heinrich: 'This is Mary McCarthy, the girl I was telling you about. She often calls to see me.'

Mary looked shyly at the man, prepared to like him because he was father of the boy she had seen on the avenue and whom she had often seen since from a distance. She felt proud because she was conscious of Ned and Bridgie and the children and the women in the caravans looking on and wondering how she was so great with such important quality. And the man was shaking her hand. It was the first time she had been treated thus by one of the quality.

'Gi's a penny.' A tousled-haired little boy sidled up to Carmel.

'Go away, Davy, and have some manners,' Mary commanded.

Timber cracked as Ned McCarthy, sullenly intent on ignoring the Obermeyers, split a log with a hand-axe. The wood sizzled when he threw it on the fire. Near a hedge a small girl appeared, as if out of a burrow, her only attire a navel-length white vest.

'Good God, where did she come from?' Heinrich exclaimed.

'Ann, get back in. Didn't I tell you not to come out with that cold?' In obedience to her sister, the girl turned round and seemed to disappear into the earth. It was then that Heinrich spotted the tent. He had overlooked it previously because of the camouflage effect of its brown-green canvas. He asked, 'Is she sick?'

'She suffers with her chest.'

'But surely that's not a suitable place for a sick child,' said Carmel indignantly.

'She can breathe better there than in the caravan. Anyway, it's not as bad as the place we were last year. The water used to come up through the ground.'

Carmel shivered when she saw the rat. It darted past the tent and into a ditch, easily eluding the yelping, emaciated dogs. One dog drew Heinrich's attention: black, it had the streamlined body of a greyhound, but its head was large and shaggy. A mythological creature, he mused. It squirmed towards them, tail wagging, but growled through bared fangs when Heinrich reached out to pat it.

'Have you any clothes or anything?' queried Mary, shooing away the dog.

'Not at the moment,' said Carmel. 'Heinrich, we had better be going.'

When they had left the camp behind, Carmel complained, 'You know what annoys me? You try to be friends with them, but they always end up begging.'

Bloodhounds, snarling, slavering, straining on leashes. Wood splintering under axes. Child, pale, trembling, silent, being yanked up through floorboards. Eyes, innocent, pleading, fixed on him. Crack of a Schmeisser. Child crumples. Head gone, eyes remain. Wide-eyed, unblinking, accusing, following him.

'Heinrich! You've kicked the blankets and sheets on to the floor.'

'What?'

'I hope your nightmares aren't starting again.'

Chapter 6

'Any other business?' asked Councillor Dempsey, Chairman of Fernboro Town Council, glaring over the top of gold-framed spectacles and defying anyone to answer in the affirmative. The ancient wall-clock had wheezed, reminding him to consult his watch, which he extracted by its silver chain from his waistcoat. God Almighty! Half-past nine! High time to bring the Council's November meeting to a close. Two hours were long enough for any meeting, but there remained one item, a very important item, the votes of sympathy. As always, when this stage was reached, he prayed that they would remember every family that had been bereaved since the Council's previous meeting. One had to be particularly careful at this time of year because more people died with the onset of harsh weather. He glanced to his right, at the sheaf of papers in front of Jack Power, the Town Clerk. Good man, Jack. He had, as usual, made a list. Jack was a great man for reading the death notices. But what's this? That upstart Lehane is saying something.

'Mr Chairperson...'

Councillor Dempsey winced: he detested these fanciful new terms which, he believed, were the result of allowing women into public life. There was even a woman on the Council—Philomena Maher, her painted Jezebel face marring the dignity of the proceedings.

'...I beg your indulgence to raise a matter that I can only describe as appalling,' continued Councillor Lehane sepulchrally. Like most politicians he had a Richter scale of words: shameful, disgraceful, utterly disgraceful, intolerable, outrageous. All these he had considered. Judging by the attentive silence of his colleagues, 'appalling' had been a good choice and he was pleased to see Mossie Kenneally, the reporter, scribbling furiously. Before the meeting he had told Mossie that he would be saying something worth printing but without specifying what it would be.

Councillor Lehane had fretted with impatience while the agenda was laboriously disposed of. He could have tabled a motion, but that would have forewarned his fellow-Councillors, given them an opening to steal some of his ammunition.

He had one moment of panic, when Councillor Fahy, seated opposite him, mentioned River Road. Councillor Lehane's knuckles whitened around his pen, but he sighed with relief when Fahy, the last of a long line of War of Independence veterans on the Council, went on to call for repairs to a footpath in the area. Fahy made the same unsuccessful call at every Council meeting.

Councillor Lehane wanted to be the first to broach this particular issue and he particularly wanted to upstage Councillor Dooley. Dooley, in Councillor Lehane's opinion, had been born with a silver spoon in his mouth and thought the world owed him a favour. High-complexioned—he could well afford the brandy—in a fawn Crombie with brown leather buttons, he was seated here at the same table at which he made money from the misfortune of others. Councillor Dooley was a solicitor, and the Town Council chamber doubled as the local courtroom.

For the Council meeting, the Chairman, the Town Clerk and Town Engineer sat behind a desk, on a dais. Behind them, higher again, was the judge's bench, which was overlooked by a brass harp attached to the wall. Opposite the bench and dais was the dock. Wooden seating for the public and the gardai—occasionally the jury sat there as well —rose in tiers, as if in an amphitheatre, encircling the lawyers' table around which were now ranged the Councillors. The press table, that tonight was ocupied solely by Mossie Kenneally, was carved out of the seating on the right side of the courtroom as one faced the judge's bench. The witness-box, pulpit-shaped, was opposite the press table.

The only light came from a bulb that oscillated gently from the ceiling on a long flex, so that shadows advanced and retreated on the room's perimeter.

Dooley and Lehane were members of the same party and were on first name terms.

They loathed each other.

Their rivalry was sharpened by the rumour that McDonald, Fernboro's septuagenarian TD, would retire before the next election, if he didn't die first.

Oliver Dooley was convinced, and he tried to convince others, that his claim to a seat in the Dáil amounted almost to a right of succession. His family had been associated with the party since its foundation and had supported it when it was at its lowest ebb. He was in his second term on the Town Council and was also a member of the County Council. His political future had seemed secure until Lehane slithered on to the scene. The most galling aspect of the whole affair was that he had initially encouraged Lehane to enter public life. Who'd have thought that Lehane would turn out to be such a snake in the grass? An opportunist with no respect for the traditions of the party, cynically using it to advance his fortunes, for he was no more than a lowly technician in a food-processing factory.

Liam Lehane often indulged in a dream: of himself alighting from a state-owned Mercedes, its door respectfully held open. Mr Liam Lehane, TD., Minister for Lands. That had a nice ring to it, though he wouldn't quibble at any portfolio. Even a parliamentary secretaryship would do for a start. He had got a foothold on the ladder and he was determined to climb. He was only twenty-seven, more than fifteen years younger than Dooley, and the party, all the political parties, were strong on youth.

Unknown to Dooley, Councillor Lehane had been coached by McDonald. 'You need a peg on which to hang your hat,' McDonald had counselled him. 'Look for an issue, and when you've got it, squeeze it. Squeeze it dry like an orange.'

On another occasion, McDonald said, 'A successful politician is an octopus. He has tentacles in every corner.'

Councillor Lehane had a tentacle into Tuohy Place whence, like a telephone cable, it conveyed information about the impending petition.

At the Tuohy Place end of the line was Jim Walsh, a member of River Road Residents' Association, who firmly believed that Lehane was responsible for getting him a Council house. Lehane didn't disabuse him of this belief, erroneous because Councillors had no function in allocating houses. All that mattered to him was that Walsh's sense of obligation had produced dividends. Councillor Lehane was convinced that at last he had an issue worth squeezing.

'I am referring to what is happening on River Road,' he said. 'As a public representative I hold it to be my duty to defend the interests of the people of Fernboro regardless of politics, creed, or social status, and that is what I intend doing in this instance. Indeed it is what I have done since coming into public life. I will speak out fearlessly and unequivocally on this issue.'

'You will not speak good, bad, or indifferent unless I decide that you are in accordance with standing orders,' exclaimed Councillor Dempsey, pushing up his spectacles.

'The people of River Road will draw their own conclusions if you prevent a discussion, Mr Chairperson,' Councillor Lehane retorted.

'This is an important matter, Mr Chairman. With due respect, I think you should allow my colleague to continue with his statement,' said Councillor Dooley, pretending to knowledge that he didn't possess.

'Very well,' Councillor Dempsey said irritably. Staring down at Councillor Lehane, he warned, 'Don't keep us here all night.'

'And cut out the claptrap!' said Councillor Slattery, the Council's only non-party member.

'Thank you for allowing me to continue, Mr Chairperson,' said Councillor Lehane. 'I know you want me to be brief, but it is difficult to be brief when the security and welfare of so many people are under threat.'

There was a rustle as Mossie Kenneally turned a page of his notebook, and Councillor Lehane paused. Fixing Lehane with bleary eyes, Councillor Slattery thumped the table, knocking Councillor Fahy's pipe from the ashtray, and roared, 'Piss or button your fly!'

Councillor Dempsey banged on a toadstool-shaped brass bell. 'Order! Order! Councillor Slattery, I would remind you that there is a lady present.'

Mossie Kenneally's shorthand was exercised to capacity.

Councillor Lehane resumed. 'If I may be allowed to speak without rude interruptions…I find myself with the serious responsibility, from which I don't shrink, of making representations on behalf of the residents of River Road who are living in daily, and indeed, nightly fear of itinerants. Furthermore, and it grieves me to have to say so, the blame for this appalling situation lies largely at the door of this Council. The itinerants are squatting on a piece of ground that the Council acquired for road-widening purposes, but this work was not done. Instead we have provided a camp-site for undesirables.'

Councillor Dempsey consulted the Town Engineer. 'Mr Fennell, have you anything to say about this?'

TJ Fennell took a last drag from a cigarette, which he then stubbed out slowly. He had much on his mind, private and Council business, and they usually overlapped. Because of the possible clash of interests, Council regulations forbade him to have private clients. Though he ate the cake from both sides, he didn't consider himself greedy. He felt he couldn't be expected to exist on the pittance that the Council called a salary.

'Mr Chairman,' he drawled, 'we bought land on River Road with the long-term aim of removing an acute bend. Funds for the work are not immediately available.' (He omitted to inform the Council that he had diverted the necessary funds to a road-making project at Fern Heights in order to facilitate the building plans of Ted Corkery, one of his best clients.)

Several Councillors spoke at once and the clock, ignored, wheezed ten. From his breast pocket Councillor Dempsey removed a neatly folded white handkerchief and mopped his brow. His voice was plaintive. 'Have you no respect for the chair? No, Councillor Lehane, you've had your say. Councillor Dooley has the floor.'

'Mr Chairman, Mr Chairman!' said Councillor Crotty. 'You are bringing politics into this. In all fairness, someone from our side of the table should be heard at this stage.' (Councillor Crotty belonged to a different party from that of Councillors Dempsey, Lehane, and Dooley.)

Councillor Dempsey reddened and fumed. 'That is poppycock. I always leave politics outside the door of this chamber. Councillor Dooley has the floor.'

'Mr Chairman, I too am speaking on behalf of the residents of River Road,' improvised Councillor Dooley. 'One can only too readily imagine what these unfortunate people are enduring, their health endangered by carrion crows and rodents, their civic order disturbed, their property rights infringed. It is, I submit, incumbent on us as Councillors to exercise our powers to the utmost in a committed effort to ameliorate their plight. Indeed, the pertinent question is: what are our statutory powers in this matter?'

'You're a solicitor; you should know,' growled Councillor Slattery.

Councillor Crotty decided to hop a ball. 'You're a painter, Councillor Slattery, but we don't expect you to bring your paint and brushes to the meeting,' he quipped.

'At least painting is better than soliciting.'

'Gentlemen, gentlemen!' pleaded Councillor Dempsey. 'Yes, Councillor Fahy?'

The War of Independence veteran, tobacco ashes on his lapels, voice scratchy, embarked upon a much-mimicked monologue. 'I am the longest serving member of the Fernboro Town Council and...' And so on, and on and on '...and I have known the travellers since I was a boy and that's not today or yesterday and I have nothing against them. You can't expect them to change their ways; you can't force them to be the same as the rest of us.'

It was then that Councillor Lehane destroyed his political prospects, though he didn't realise this at the time. 'Hitler had the right idea,' he declared.

Councillor McGowan, seated at the end of the table, facing the Chairman, pounced. 'That remark shows Councillor Lehane in his true colours—a political opportunist and fascist.'

Councillor Lehane: 'I don't take my orders from Moscow.'

Councillor McGowan was a member of a recently established socialist party and although he had thrown the term "fascist" at Councillor Lehane, he viewed the River Road issue pragmatically rather than ideologically. Itinerants, he reminded himself, don't vote; River Road residents do. He kicked for touch.

'Mr Chairman,' he said, 'while I have every sympathy with the people of River Road, I think at this stage that we have inadequate information on the matter. Therefore I propose that the Town Clerk prepare a full report for our next monthly meeting.'

Councillor Slattery belched, sending beer fumes into the air. Councillor Crotty, reminded of the imminence of pub closing-time, said quickly, 'I second that proposal.'

Councillor Lehane said, 'I would agree with having a report, providing that everything is done in the meantime to alleviate the appalling...'

'Yes, yes, Councillor Lehane, we already know your views,' said Councillor Dempsey. Turning to the Town Clerk, he asked, 'Mr Power, do you foresee any difficulties in preparing a report?'

'No, Mr Chairman, I don't envisage any great difficulties,' Mr Power replied, 'but there are some points involved that I shall have to clarify with our legal adviser.'

'Very well,' said Councillor Dempsey. 'Is the proposal adopted? Fine. Now we can go on to votes of sympathy.'

Chapter Seven

There was a knock on the door and it opened. 'May I come in?' said Heinrich.

Eamonn put the open book, cover upwards, on the bed. 'Sit down here,' he said, clearing the schoolbooks from the chair. He seated himself on the side of the bed, feet on the floor.

'Can you turn that thing down a bit?'

Eamonn leaned towards the locker and turned off the transistor.

'Are you studying hard?' asked Heinrich, surveying the room. When last had he been in here: six months ago, a year? It must be a year at least. Certainly he would have noticed that calendar girl in a minuscule bikini, sipping a soft drink. Over the bed was a large poster of a rock group. The wardrobe door was slightly ajar, revealing a guitar; trousers, a shirt and tie, components of a school uniform, hung from a peg on the room door.

'The real grind doesn't start until after Christmas,' said Eamonn.

'That reminds me—would you like to go to Bavaria? Franz has invited us over for Christmas.'

Candles, real candles on trees, lit Eamonn's memory of a Christmas in Bavaria, and he smelled roast goose and tasted mulled wine. Bavaria: visits to lakes and mountains, his cousins fussing over him, in raptures over his accent, and above all the trips to Munich, to the big shops with his aunt Hilda who told everyone that he was *mein braver Knabe aus Irland* and bought him anything he wanted.

But he was only a child then and Hilda was dead now and the cousins scattered. If he went to Bavaria, he'd be looking at middle-aged and elderly people, and he would be wondering. He said, 'I'd prefer to stay here.'

'Oh, I thought you enjoyed visiting Germany.'

'I did, years ago.'

'What changed your mind?'

The self-righteous sensibility of youth surfaced in Eamonn. He reached behind him, then turned like an avenging angel towards his father and exclaimed, 'This!'

Heinrich didn't take the book; its contents were only too obvious from the title. 'Yes, yes, your mother told me you were reading a lot about those...those things.'

Eamonn found the page he was seeking. Pointing to a photograph, he thrust the book at his father. 'Those things! Those *things*! Is that what you call it?' The photograph showed corpses stacked on a truck, shrivelled, cropped heads facing heavenwards.

Again Heinrich declined to take the book. Pages fluttering, it fell on the carpet. The pages subsided, leaving the photograph exposed. Heinrich pushed back his chair. The book lay between him and Eamonn.

'I do not need pictures to tell me what happened.'

Eamonn looked sharply at his father. 'What do you mean? Were you inside a camp?'

'No, I was not in a camp.' At least that is the truth, Heinrich thought, but he didn't meet his son's eyes.

A train rattled over the viaduct, making the sash window tremble. The goods train from Dublin. Heinrich's mind shifted forward. It should be carrying the machine part he had ordered from Germany. He would call to the railway station first thing in the morning.

'I just thought that you might have been in one and that that's the reason you prefer not to talk about it,' persisted Eamonn.

'Is reading about it not enough?'

'I get angry when I'm reading—and ashamed. You know, when you think of Germany with all its great poets and composers and scientists.'

Heinrich rose from his chair, moved to his right, and stood with his back to Eamonn. 'Has your mother no objection to that?' he asked, pointing to the calendar, trying to keep his voice light.

'She doesn't like it,' replied Eamonn, retrieving the book from the floor. He closed the book but kept it in his hands. He added, 'I suppose you're right. There's not much point in talking about it.'

Heinrich faced his son again. 'Eamonn, I did not say that, but you should not allow those books to distort your view of Germany. The Third Reich is gone.'

'But it's important to remember.'

'You read that somewhere. But when did remembering ever prevent a recurrence of evil?'

'But why? How could a nation like Germany do it?'

'My God, how often I have asked myself that question.' Heinrich pulled the chair nearer the bed and sat down again. 'I have thought, I have read innumerable books by historians, philosophers, all sorts of experts. I have gone back over my own experiences but I cannot find an answer.'

'Maybe you are seeking an excuse as well as an answer?'

'Let me ask you a question,' Heinrich said abruptly. 'What people are important to you? Whom do you respect?'

'Well, apart from you and mother, there's Brother Mulhare, and I respect my friends. And Bob Dylan.'

'Who is Bob Dylan?'

'A singer.'

'I see. Anyway, try to imagine yourself in a situation where all these people, or almost all of of them, adopted a particular point of view, a view that was shared by the state. Would you be able to stand aloof, or want to?'

'I would stand by what was right.'

Can you be absolutely sure, Eamonn? Remember that television documentary? How you were carried away by it? Can you imagine what it was like to have been there?'

'I was just a child when I saw that documentary.'

'There were a lot of children in Germany in the 1930s, but unlike you, they did not have the benefit of hindsight.'

'But people must have known what was going on. They weren't all children.'

Heinrich tapped his son on the knee. 'Eamonn, I want to tell you a story, a true one. At the end of the war a camp guard, a woman, was set upon by the inmates—and I am not blaming them. They kicked her, between the legs, mostly. They kicked her to death. She had known, to use your expression, "what was going on", but she probably approved or disapproved of it no more than she approved or disapproved of a shower of rain or a snowstorm. No doubt she understood the desire in her attackers for retaliation and was expecting a few blows and kicks, but as the kicks continued she must have become confused and incredulous, and it is my belief that she died without really knowing why.'

'*Officers and men, you carry no personal responsibility for these measures. The responsibility rests with the Führer and me.*'

Despite the passing of three decades, Himmler's words rang as clear as ever in Heinrich's mind.

He had gone straight from Eamonn's room to the office. It was where he retreated when he wanted to be alone. The only furniture Heinrich had installed in the office, a smallish room off the hall, was a roll-top desk and leather-seated high-back chair. A glass-fronted bookcase and a Victorian print of a racehorse had been there when he bought the house.

The print, over the mantlepiece, reminded him of a horse he had seen near the itinerant camp a week before, on the day he had been walking with Carmel. The horse had stretched and stretched towards a tuft of grass but was prevented from reaching it every time by a long halter. He felt as if he too were haltered to his memories. Each year the rope lengthened, the memories receded and he seemed to be attaining a state of comfortable amnesia, until a sight, a sound, a taste, a printed word, a smell, jolted him back—to hell. His conversation with Eamonn was such a jolt.

The rumble of tanks, the clatter of half-tracks, the snarl of motor-cycles, the purr of staff cars, barked commands, booted footfalls —sounds of the German Eleventh Army trying to advance faster than rapidly approaching winter. Nikolayev, on the road to the Black Sea. Grain silos and oil tanks and shipyard cranes. And Himmler.

Heinrich looked up at another Heinrich: Heinrich Himmler. Greenish eyes magnified by thin-framed spectacles. Their eyes met. In that instant Himmler smiled, a smile as fleeting as a film-frame, but kind, and Heinrich was grateful, grateful for any sign of reassurance.

'This is an ideological battle and a struggle of the races,' said Himmler. 'Here in this struggle stands National Socialism, an ideology based on the value of our Germanic Nordic blood. On the other side stands a population of one hundred and eighty million, a mixture of races, whose very names are unpronounceable, and whose physique is such that one can shoot them down without pity or compassion. These animals that torture and ill-treat every prisoner from our side, every wounded man they come across and do not treat them the way decent soldiers would—these animals have been welded by the Jews into one religion, one ideology: Bolshevism. Despite such provocation, we Germans, who are the only people in the world with a decent attitude towards animals, will also assume a decent attitude towards these human animals, but it is a crime against our own blood to worry about them or to give them ideals.'

Typically bourgeois. A conscientious clerk. Such terms, Heinrich noted wryly in later years, were invariably used by historians and commentators to describe Himmler. But on that day in Nikolayev Himmler was a *Reichsführer* and Head of the SS and what you saw was power, black-uniformed power, creating an awesome aura around the man. And you were young and lacked standards of comparison and most of all were German and you heeded and accepted that power.

A plane thundered by and Himmler paused. The thunder faded to a drone and he resumed, 'Yours is a soldierly duty: it is nothing less than to prevent our front-line troops from being stabbed in the back. The resettlements halt the flow of information which enables the cowardly partisans to murder our heroic soldiers; and, indeed, our own special units—your brothers-in-arms—have suffered casualties at the hands of these partisan animals. You, by your actions, are also preventing the spread of diseases. My experts inform me that the ghettos are conducive to epidemics. The inhabitants of the ghettos crowd together like vermin and, of course, they do not understand our German principles of hygiene. Therefore, they must be resettled. For the present, however, (Himmler's tone became sorrowful) our great task must be treated with that tact which, thank God, is a matter of course and inherent in us Germans. This, I regret to say, is necessary because too many people still cling to outmoded, sentimental ideals. I promise you, though, that these foolish notions shall be eradicated, and when that time comes, you shall be justly rewarded. And you shall have a unique place in history.'

Heinrich parted the curtains, pulled down the window-sash, and breathed deeply. The air, moistened by the Fern, was dank. The memories persisted. Himmler dismissing the men, then testily addressing the officers...

'Gentlemen, my orders are to be obeyed to the letter! I am astounded to learn that certain resettlements, which I expressly ordered, have not yet taken place. The excuse that I have been given is that agricultural communities are involved. These sub-humans, no matter what their occupations, are an insidious source of contamination. There can be no exemptions.'

Heinrich drew the curtains and came away from the window. He sat at the desk. He heard another voice, an educated accent. Otto Ohlendorf. Little Otto, the men called him. He had been hanged years before, in 1950 or '51.

Blond and handsome in his *Gruppenführer's* uniform, he was seated immediately to Himmler's right. '*Mein Reichsführer*,' said Ohlendorf suavely, 'I am pleased to inform you that the necessary measures have been taken to comply with your order. Arrangements are complete for a special action and, perhaps, you would do us the honour of witnessing it?'

'Nothing would please me more,' Himmler replied. 'Unfortunately, however, duty requires my presence elsewhere.'

'That got rid of him—I knew he wouldn't have the stomach for it,' declared Ohlendorf after Himmler's departure.

The incredible thing was that Ohlendorf had the stomach for it, Heinrich reflected. Ohlendorf, lawyer and economist, who left an important office job in Berlin to come to Russia. Who voluntarily entered hell.

Ohlendorf, a few months later, presiding at a Christmas dinner. That was in Simferopol, and Ohlendorf made a speech in celebration of a successful action: an estimated ten thousand people had been resettled.

Heinrich routinely raised his glass to every shout of 'Prost!' Meal over, he withdrew to a terrace, away from the atmosphere thick with tobacco smoke and awash in Crimean white wine.

'*Obersturmführer*, you didn't eat much.' Ohlendorf was standing beside him.

'The climate doesn't seem to suit my appetite, *Herr Gruppenführer*.'

'Come with me.' Ohlendorf led the way down a corridor and into a room. He closed the door, shutting out the sounds of laughter and singing. Over a desk was a portrait of Hitler and on another wall was a large-scale map of the Crimea. Ohlendorf indicated a chair and told Heinrich to sit down. He removed a bottle and two glasses from a filing cabinet. 'Drink this,' he said.

Heinrich obeyed and the French brandy started to dissolve the knot at the pit of his stomach.

Ohlendorf sat on his desk, feet swinging. 'How long have you been with us?' he asked.

'Around four months, *Herr Gruppenführer*.'

'You need not be so formal in here. You and I have much in common. I've been noticing you: you seem to have difficulties in becoming reconciled to your duties?'

'I do my duty.'

'But you have reservations?'

'Well, I...'

'You can be frank with me. I assure you, I regard this as a confidential conversation between gentlemen.'

'Thank you. Yes, yes, I have some reservations.'

'I should have been disappointed if you had said otherwise.' Ohlendorf refilled Heinrich's glass. 'We have automatons who experience pleasure in carrying out actions and, I'm sorry to say, they include a number of officers. It is a trait that I abhor; it is reminiscent of school bullying. Intelligence is the quality that I seek and that I value most highly in my officers, because only the intelligent can fully comprehend the breadth of conception, the boldness of the pattern, that lies behind the policy of which we are the instruments.'

Ohlendorf went to the filing cabinet and extracted a file. 'Read this,' he said, opening the file and handing it to Heinrich.

The soldier in the Eastern Territories is not merely a fighter according to

the rules of the art of war, but he is also the bearer of a ruthless national ideology.
Therefore, the soldier must have understanding of the necessity of severe but
just revenge on sub-human Jewry.

The order was signed by Field Marshal Erich von Manstein,
Commander of the Eleventh Army.

'You seem surprised?' said Ohlendorf.

'Field Marshal von Manstein. He is one of our most able generals,
thoroughly professional...'

'No doubt that is true, but, between ourselves, he is not exactly an
ardent National Socialist. Nevertheless, as you can see, even he
recognises the necessity of our actions.'

Ohlendorf put a hand on Heinrich's shoulder. 'What we are doing
is not without precedent,' he said. 'Ironic though it may be, we have
learned from the Israelites. God ordered them to destroy their enemies,
and they did so. The precedents are numerous: the American solution
to the problem of Red Indians; the invention of concentration camps by
the British during the Boer War. And is the bombing of cities much
different from what we are engaged in?'

After his meeting with Ohlendorf, Heinrich rejoined his comrades
in their revelry, and he was soon uproariously merry.

Maybe you are seeking an excuse...No, that is not true. I do not need an
excuse. I am prepared to answer for what I did of my own free will.
Anything else is not my responsibility.

'You keep looking at the door,' said Cathal Corkery.

'Anything is better than looking at you,' quipped Eamonn.

After the conversation with his father, Eamonn no longer felt like
reading. He felt hungry. A search of his pockets uncovered almost a
pound in change, more than enough for Dino's.

There he now sat with Cathal, drinking coffee at a formica-topped
table, tomato-ketchup-spattered plates between them.

'There's not much talent around tonight,' Cathal complained.

Eamonn tacitly agreed. 'Let's split,' he said.

The girl from the camp, Mary—he had casually elicited her name from his mother—would hardly arrive at this stage. He had seen her in Dino's a few times, standing at the take-away counter. All the lads had noticed her and a lot of them said she was a fine thing. Senan Murphy said it was a pity that she was only a knacker.

Chapter 8

It was like the sudden switching off of a radio. Talk and laughter stopped when the three men entered Gradys. They seemed to be sober and were reasonably well-attired, better than some others in the premises. The wooden floor creaked as the men walked towards the counter where customers, Bill Sullivan among them, were seated on high stools. A coin dropped by unconsciously loosened fingers whirled on the card-table and a lump of coal spluttered on the fire. One of the men, who appeared to be the youngest of the trio, tugged a freckled fist from a trouser pocket. The fist unclenched, crisp notes unfurled, fivers and tenners predominating. Customers exchanged knowing looks. They awaited the next move as expectantly as if they were watching a silent film. Glasses, full and not so full, stood temporarily forgotten on the counter and table and mantelpiece and on the floor beside the form that lined the wall opposite the window.

The camera switched to Grady who was motionless behind the counter, his aproned belly bulging within a few inches of the dripping beer dispensers, purple-red face inscrutable. His right hand was out of sight, under the counter, clasped round a half-yard length of thick rubber tubing.

Bill Sullivan, like many River Road residents, went to Gradys every Saturday night, and when funds were flush, he was there at other times as well. The pub marked the junction of River Road and Bridge Street and its customers were all male. The intrepid women and girls who ventured in occasionally encountered indifference or barely concealed hostility. The good-looking ones in particular were disconcerted by the lack of response to their charms: it was as if they were trespassing on an assembly of eunuchs. When they asked for ice in their drinks, Grady, who regarded them as brazen hussies, glared at them as though they had come from the Titanic. And when they asked for the loo, he told them he had no special convenience for ladies. That usually did the trick. In blushing confusion they would retreat to one of Fernboro's several garish new lounge bars. But the pub had two resident females: Annie Grady who, when not playing Forty-Five, the card game to which she was addicted, assisted her brother by washing glasses in a zinc basin under a cold tap; and Soot, an aged white-and-tan terrier whose fur was singed from lying too close to the fire.

Annie was a few years younger than her brother, who was in his late sixties. Their pub was really a club and most of the clientele, a mixture of farmers and workers and pensioners, had inherited their membership rights. Each newcomer unknowingly served an apprenticeship. If he displayed the slightest tendency towards rowdiness, his indentures were cancelled: others were served before him, and when he did get a drink he found himself alone, excluded from all conversations; and if he succeeded in infiltrating a card-game, the rest of the players ganged up on him.

It was only after he'd moved to Tuohy Place that Bill Sullivan began to frequent the pub, eased into it by Jim Walsh, who was a regular patron. Bill's carpenter's eye appreciated the hand-crafted marble-top counter, the bottle-packed shelves inlaid with two mirrors in ornate gilt frames, and he enjoyed watching Grady tipping out spirits from pewter measures. Often, Grady discarded the measures and filled a glass straight from the bottle: a lifetime in the trade had made him an expert calculator of doubles and half-ones. And, of course, Bill approved of Grady's practice of being generous to the customers in matters of the spirit, mostly whiskey.

Grady, in Bill's fancy, resembled an amiable frog, although his ample belly was deceptive, for he was teetotal, as was Annie who was tall and angular. Avarice wasn't as pronounced in Grady as in the majority of publicans, and he'd give you a drink on the slate and quite frequently treat you to one on the house.

Though few, the house rules were strict: no more drink when Grady said you'd had enough; no higher stakes at cards than fivepence all-in; all must contribute to the regular singing sessions (a recitation, no matter how brief, was acceptable from non-singers); singers not to be interrupted except for the purpose of joining the chorus and prompting; and, finally, Soot's place by the fire was inviolable.

The silent film became a talkie. 'Give us three pints,' said Ned McCarthy, slapping the wad of notes on the counter. Stools scraped the floor as customers manoeuvred away from him and his companions.

'We don't serve your sort here,' Grady said curtly. He stepped back from the beer dispensers but kept his hand under the counter.

'Why not?'

'You're wasting your time arguing.'

'Is my money not good enough?'

'You'll get no drink here.'

Grady looked at Bill Sullivan. 'Bill, I see you're nearly empty there,' he said. 'Another pint?'

Bill nodded. Grady picked up a clean glass with his left hand. He put the glass under a dispenser. 'Give us a half-one,' shouted someone from the card table. Throats were cleared, stout was gulped from froth-ringed glasses, cigarettes were lit, Annie shuffled the cards, the dog scratched behind an ear, the backdoor latch clicked as men shuttled to relieve themselves.

But the activity and talk were constrained. Customers had joined the cast, ham-actors in a jerky old movie.

Still the three men stayed in the premises, in it but not of it, islanded. From the fire that was more than a match for the frosty weather came waves of heat, but they experienced no warmth. Fresh, cream-collared pints were near, yet tantalisingly out of reach.

Antennae seemed to bristle on Tom McCarthy's wiry-haired head as he turned his back to the counter. From left to right the antennae began sweeping the premises, then halted. Tom's countenance brightened, a screen flickering to life. He had recognised a face. 'Hardy weather, Mr Ahern.'

Peter Ahern, eyes fixed on the floor, grunted.

Tom tried again. 'You'll have a drink, sir?' he asked ingratiatingly.

'No, I have enough.'

Notes were sandwiched between Ned McCarthy's palm and the counter. Mikey Driscoll touched his elbow. 'Come on, Ned,' he said softly, 'we won't get notten here.'

'You can go if you want to. I'm staying until I get a fuckin' drink,' shouted Ned. He banged the counter. Notes scattered on the floor.

Grady tightened his grip on the rubber tubing.

Ned's glance swept around the pub. Each customer hoped that the glance wouldn't rest on him. 'Aren't we human beings like the rest of ye?' he challenged.

'Get out or I'll call the guards,' hissed Grady.

'Ah, don't do that, sir,' pleaded Tom, rising from the floor where he had been retrieving the money.

Ned took the notes from his father and replaced them on the counter. 'Will you give us a drink to bring away?' he said.

'Will you go if I do?' Grady said.

'We will, sir,' agreed Tom.

At Grady's request, Annie went to the kitchen. She returned with a cardboard box and went behind the counter. Into the box, following Ned's instructions, she put pint and half-pint bottles of stout, flagons of cider, and noggin bottles of whiskey.

'Will that be all?' said Grady, mental arithmetic creasing his forehead.

'Give us a Babby Power.'

Annie handed a baby bottle of whiskey to Ned who placed it in a coat pocket. He shoved the notes across the counter. 'Take what you want,' he said.

Grady seized a tenner and fiver. He rooted for change in the till.

Mikey carried the box to the door, which was held open by Tom. Icy air sneaked in. They went out.

Ned pocketed his change. When he got outside the door he paused. He listened. The volume of talk inside the door was increasing. The radio was being turned up. Someone laughed. Mockingly, thought Ned. He screwed the cap off the baby bottle of whiskey. Through the door he burst.

'I'll get you the jail, I'll get you the jail,' screamed Grady, brandishing the rubber tubing.

Ned put the bottle to his lips, tilted back his head, drained the whiskey. His throat burned, his eyes watered. He felt good. As good or better than anyone. He arched his right arm. Grady and the customers on the stools ducked. The bottle shattered on the edge of the counter.

'You can do what you fuckin' well like now!' crowed Ned, whiskey-hoarse.

'Shush!' said Grady, putting a finger to pursed lips.

Jim Walsh got up from the card-table, went to the window, and eased back an edge of the blind.

Doors banged. An engine spluttered and then ran smoothly. Its noise receded. 'They've gone,' Jim confirmed.

There was a flurry of orders. Annie Grady swept glass fragments into a dustpan.

The smashing of the bottle had reassured Bill Sullivan: it confirmed his opinion that itinerants were a sneaky, dangerous crowd. Though he couldn't prove it, he was certain they had stolen tools belonging to him from a building site a few years before. He had spent a long, dry time getting the money together to replace the tools. However, before the bottle was thrown, he had, despite himself, felt a surge of sympathy for Ned McCarthy and his companions: they were, after all, only looking for a few pints.

Grady skimmed froth off the top of a pint with a breadknife. 'One of them seemed to know you well,' he said to Peter Ahern.

'Aye, he was up with me looking for straw. He told me a sob-story about needing the straw to make mattresses for the tents.'

'Did you give him some?'

'Indeed I didn't. I wouldn't have any truck with him or any of them. I got rid of him as fast as I could. Having them around the place is asking for trouble. They scout first and then steal.'

Jim Walsh was reseated at the card-table. 'At least you got their money,' he said to Grady.

'And I nearly got my head knocked off with a bottle,' Grady retorted. 'Anyway, I might as well have their money as some other publican.'

No matter which way Mary McCarthy turned, the frost stung. It bit her nose and she pulled the blanket over her face, then it attacked her toes and she tucked in her sock-clad feet. And she was bursting. She uncovered her eyes. Through an opening in the tent-flap she could see a star, far away, cold. She knew she was only postponing the inevitable, but she dreaded having to crawl out from between Davy and Ann, from underneath the blankets and topcoat. Careful of her steps, she'd go behind the hedge and she'd fumble with stiff fingers at her clothes. Even the thought of it was enough to make you shiver. But it could be worse; she could be having her monthlies. And she supposed it would be still worse if you were pregnant.

She shouldn't have had that mug of cider. Now she was paying the price. She shouldn't have drunk at all, or else have drunk a lot more, enough to fall into a dead sleep. The drink was really flowing tonight —Ned had sold a horse—and Lukey, whose wedding was only a few weeks away, had also brought some. She came away because Mikey Driscoll was there. Anyway she was nervous when there was that much drink around.

Frost stabbed her kidneys from the inside, or so it felt to Mary. She'd have to go. She slipped on shoes. She crawled from the tent, out on to rock-hard soil that chilled her hands and knees. Murmurs came from the camp-fire, which was about twenty yards away. Mary recognised her mother's laughter which, when she was drunk, was close to a shriek. The earth glistened and hedges bared hoared ribs.

Mary stood up. Behind her the ground crackled. Her shoulders were grabbed and she was spun around. 'There you are, Miss High-and-Mighty!'

Mikey Driscoll spat out the words, his alcohol-sour breath blasting Mary. She averted her head. 'Let me go! You'll wake the childer.'

'You think you're too good for me, is that it?'

The slap across her face sent Mary staggering against the tent. 'That'll learn you, you bitch,' roared Mikey. He reeled towards the camp-fire.

Tears of rage and pain almost blinded Mary. She rubbed her eyes. 'Hitting women! That's all you're good for, you dirty bastard,' she screeched.

Maggie McCarthy shrieked in sympathy with her daughter and swayed against Julia Driscoll, Mikey's mother. Fingers entangled in each other's hair, the two women rolled within perilous range of the fire, locked in battle.

Men and women, McCarthys and Driscolls, joined the fray which, like a vortex, then sucked in other inhabitants of the campsite, Butlers and Quilligans and Walls. Dogs, tails between legs, cowered under carts and vans and behind caravans. In the caravans children cried, their cries drowned in the cacophony of breaking bottles and screams and shouts and blows and slaps. Bluish flames from spilled whiskey flared and died on the fire.

Mary crouched near the tent, Davy and Ann, one on each side, pressed close to her. Davy and Ann were fearful but spellbound by the actions of the marionette-like figures in the firelight: flaying, seemingly disjointed limbs tangling and disentangling and falling in heaps as if someone had cut a string.

Unlike the younger children, Mary viewed the scene with detachment, almost dispassionately. Her ire at Mikey Driscoll had subsided quickly. To her, violent rows, like begging, were an integral part of existence. But she remained on her hunkers: bitter experience had taught her that the only way of avoiding involvement was to stay out of sight of the protagonists. Neutrality wasn't recognised in a fight amongst travellers. Once you were in the arena, be it campsite, pub or street, you were expected to enter the fray, your participation encouraged by insults, punches, kicks.

A woman howled, a howl of anguish and anger rising to the stars. Mary crouched lower.

———————

The howl sent a tremor through Helen Moran. Years ago she had seen a woman's skull being split open with an ashplant during a tinkers' fight.

The hot-water bottle on which Helen's feet rested was tepid. The luminous numerals on the bedside clock recorded twenty minutes past midnight. She had retired early with the intention of getting up for first Mass, seven-thirty on a Sunday.

'You stinking whore. I'll brain ya!'

The words were so distinct that it seemed to Helen that they'd been uttered directly underneath her bedroom window. A thwack cracked like a rifle shot. She felt sick. The prayers she recited automatically failed to counteract her sense of vulnerability. She listened for every sound from the camp. There'd been rows before, but never as bad as this.

She got out of bed and dressed rapidly. She didn't switch on the light. It was better not to run the risk of attracting their attention, though she knew it was unlikely that they'd bother with her. Still, if tinkers thought you were interfering, they'd close ranks and turn on you.

Pursued by the din from the camp, Helen hurried out her front door and down River Road. The din lessened only when she turned into River View Drive. She pressed hard on the doorbell and almost fell into Joe Murphy's arms. He assisted her, pale and trembling, into the hallway.

'It's terrible...the camp...I think they're killing one another up there.'

'Don't be upset, Mrs Moran—you're among friends. I'll ring the gardai.'

'What's wrong?' asked Sandra Murphy, entering the hallway. Her gaze fell on Helen's slippered feet. 'You'll get your death of cold,' she said. 'Come into the kitchen and I'll make a cup of tea.'

'Drive slowly past the camp,' said Garda Keogh to his partner, Garda Breen.

As the squad car's speed slackened, Garda Keogh rolled down a window. He could hear someone yelling. For an instant the car's headlamps spotlighted Mary McCarthy and Davy and Ann.

'It must be awful for the children,' said Garda Breen.

'They get hardened to it,' said Garda Keogh, 'though I often think that the children should be taken away from them. It would be one way of solving the problem.' He put on his well worn peaked cap, and added, 'Turn around here. When we stop beside the camp leave the engine running. I don't believe we'll have any trouble but it's wise not to take any chances. Knackers can be treacherous. And let me do the talking.'

At the camp, Garda Keogh got out of the car. The door was ajar, shielding the lower part of his body; his left foot was inside the car, his left elbow on the car roof, and his right hand was in a trouser pocket, a deep pocket, a receptacle for a baton.

'What the hell is going on here?' he shouted authoritatively.

'Notten, Guard, 'tis a thing a notten', replied a voice from the direction of the dying fire.

Into the circle of dancing bluish light from the beacon atop the patrol car shuffled Tom McCarthy. Dark streaks converged in a blotch around his mouth. ''Tis yourself, Garda Keogh.'

'I have enough to be doing without wasting time on you. You'll find yourself before a judge if you're not careful.' Garda Keogh spoke as if he were admonishing a recalcitrant child.

'Don't worry yourself, Guard—'tis all over. 'Twas only the drink.'

'Is that blood on your face?' queried Garda Breen through the open window of the driver's door.

Tom rubbed his mouth. He seemed surprised by the resultant stain on his hand.

'Does anyone need a doctor?' added Garda Breen.

Garda Keogh sat into the car, slamming the door. 'Drive on, for Jasus sake,' he exclaimed.

As they headed towards town, he said irritably, 'Didn't I tell you to let me do the talking?'

'But supposing somebody was hurt...'

Garda Keogh flung his cap into the rear seat. 'Listen,' he commanded, 'you can't afford to be soft with knackers. Give them the smallest opening and they'll ride you.'

Chapter 9

'If they don't go, I'll have to go. I can't stand it much longer. My nerves are at breaking point. I'll go to Dublin to my daughter.'

'That won't be necessary, Mrs Moran,' said Joe Murphy. 'You are among friends here and we won't tolerate a situation where anyone is forced from her home.'

Heinrich's compassion for Mrs Moran was diluted by his annoyance at what he regarded as Joe's clumsy attempt at emotional blackmail through the exploitation of her obvious distress. It was well over a week since Joe's previous visit to the Obermeyer house, and as each day passed Heinrich became more confident that he would not call again, at least not in connection with the petition. Now he realised that that had been wishful thinking: Murphy was not the type to be put off so easily.

As for the petition, Carmel had mentioned it casually, suggesting that they should perhaps sign it for the sake of good neighbourly relations. Heinrich had replied that they probably would not have to bother about it one way or the other.

'I'll put a fresh sup in this,' said Carmel, taking Helen's teacup.

'Did you see *The Fernboro News* report of the Town Council meeting?' Joe asked.

Heinrich had seen the report: its tone and particularly Councillor

Lehane's contribution, had reminded him of things he had hoped to forget.

'Matters are coming to a head,' Joe continued. 'The Council will have to find a solution once the petition is submitted and it will be submitted as soon as we have the final few names.'

'Has everyone signed?' said Carmel.

'All but yourselves and Mr Fitzharris. Do you know him? He used to live in your side of the country. An odd sort of man.' Joe didn't wait for Carmel to reply. He looked at Heinrich. 'Well, have you come to a decision?'

———————

'Have you decided, Oberleutnant?'

Dust caked the many lines in Colonel Reinhart's grim strong-featured face, and dulled his close-clipped grey hair. His headquarters were in the remains of the village's sole stone building. One wall was gone, and so was the roof. All around was the brown steppe and from the east came the muffled thunder of artillery.

Heinrich had made a decision: there appeared to be only one way of avoiding disgrace, or worse.

The previous night he had curled in a patch of feathery grass, which was made to seem as comfortable as a mattress by over three months of accumulated weariness.

He had entered Russia on 22 June 1941, invasion day. Though glorying in its victories, he viewed the German army, and therefore himself, as a liberator, not a conqueror, an opinion reinforced by the spectacle of Soviet citizens throwing flowers at him and his comrades and pressing platters of food on them.

Time and space became distorted. Heinrich marched and fought and was ferried on tanks for kilometre after kilometre, and yet it was as if he weren't moving at all. On and on the plain stretched, merging with the sky. And the landmarks supplied by the war were always the same: contorted bodies, the blackened hulks of tanks, twisted gun-metal, heaped rubble. He saw the steppe, like a floor stripped of a carpet, losing its buttercups and purple hyacinths, and the nights were lengthening, the sun cooling, so he knew that time was passing, but it was not chronometric time.

'Oberleutnant. Oberleutnant Obermeyer!' Heinrich felt a hand on his right shoulder, shaking him. 'Oberleutnant, get up! At once!'

Heinrich leaped from the grass and sprang to attention.

Gunflashes lit the south-eastern sky behind Captain Raspe, who demanded, 'Do you realise what time it is? You should have started inspection of forward posts an hour ago.'

Next morning Heinrich was ordered to report to Colonel Reinhart. 'I should not have to tell you that failure to inspect our forward posts could have the gravest consequences,' the Colonel said.

'Sir, I can only say that my behaviour was out of character.' Inwardly Heinrich cursed Raspe. He should have realised that he would report him. Raspe had never forgotten that occasion when he had overheard Heinrich mimicking his proletarian accent. He pretended not to have heard, but his countenance betrayed him. And he had heard the laughter.

'Hauptmann Raspe is...how shall I put it?...enthusiastic,' said Colonel Reinhart.

That was putting it mildly, Heinrich thought. Raspe yearned to shoot summarily every captured Russian officer: he claimed they were all political commissars. But Raspe was courageous. It was galling having to admit it but he was.

'He wants to press charges against you,' continued Colonel Reinhart. 'I'm sure I don't have to spell out the possible consequences.'

Heinrich was cold, bone-marrow cold. The Obermeyers disgraced? Their name, once proud, besmirched? His parents. Uncle Walter. And what would his friends think? What would they say? Then Heinrich had an idea. He said, 'Sir, I am available for an assignment.'

'God in heaven, man, spare me the heroics.' Colonel Reinhart rubbed his tired, pouched eyes as if to quench the anger that had sparked there. His voice regained its characteristic temperate pitch. 'There are, I am informed, special units of commandos that set a very high value on trained officers. I am unaware of the exact function of these commandos, but I gather that they are generously rewarded for whatever it is that they do. If you should volunteer for the commandos, and this is only a suggestion, I believe that Raspe—Hauptmann Raspe —can be persuaded to modify his position.'

Heinrich became conscious of the sun's warmth.

A few hours later—he had been allowed time to make up his mind—Heinrich was back with the Colonel. 'Yes, sir, I have decided.'

Within a week Heinrich was in the special commandos, and within days of joining them he was desperately regretting his decision. But he had to stay and obey or be shot. Or so he was led to believe. Many times, when it was too late, he wished that he had disobeyed: in the commandos you lost something incalculably more precious than life. You lost your soul. As for disgrace: in the commandos disgrace was honour and honour was disgrace.

A question, a suspicion, tormented Heinrich. Had Colonel Reinhart known more about the commandos than he had admitted? No, surely not. Still, whom could you trust? Whom could you believe? Was there anything, any truth, worth believing in? But surely the Colonel, an old soldier, a World War One veteran, would, if he knew the full facts, never sanction such a fate for one of his officers.

Heinrich's pay trebled because he was a commando. His vodka ration, though generous, was now inadequate and he supplemented it. He was entitled to home leave every three months. On three occasions he didn't go all the way home: he got as far as Munich where he stayed out of sight in the room, mostly the bed, of a professional woman whose expertise, along with alcohol, induced in him forgetfulness.

On the one occasion he did go all the way home, he was gripped by a vindictive feeling towards his parents. He found himself snubbing his mother whose hurt, confused reaction perversely pleased him. But his pleasure would quickly vanish, to be replaced by shame and sincere repentance. He could not understand his own behaviour: it was as though he were a mouthpiece for a ventriloquist with a warped sense of humour. He discovered that he despised his father, whom he wanted to shock out of what Heinrich regarded as a smug, religious-orientated world in which right and wrong were conveniently placed antithetically. His father sensed Heinrich's mood and, unlike most people, never asked him what things were 'really like' in Russia.

In later years, Heinrich often wondered if anybody would have believed him had he answered that question truthfully. Orders had bound him to silence, but had orders been the real reason for his reticence? Or had he hidden the truth to avoid self-incrimination?

Would people have appreciated hearing the truth? He thought not.

They probably would have resented him for telling it. Anyway, he reasoned, if he had revealed what was really happening in Russia and people had believed him, they would have found some means of explaining it away. Even if they had not, if they had been horrified and shamed, would it have made any difference?

A new (Aryan) name was on the big drapery store in Leopold Street owned by Adela Ornstein's family: the name of a man whom Heinrich remembered as an employee in the business. Adela and her parents weren't there one morning. Nobody knew where they had gone, and nobody had enquired. Heinrich preferred not to think about the matter. Besides, he wasn't short of female company during that home leave.

Most of his male contemporaries were away; some were dead. Ernst Hinterberger, already a captain, was in the Sixth Army, approaching Stalingrad. Ernst and thousands of fighting troops abandoned to bullets and bombs and snow and starvation and slavery whilst privileges were showered on the commandos, whose direst enemy was alcoholism. Heinrich recalled bitterly that many of the commandos could not even shoot straight at stationary targets, stationary save for spasms of naked, literally naked, fear.

'Yes, Joe, I have come to a decision.'

'And?'

'I cannot sign.'

Carmel tried in vain to catch Heinrich's eye. Helen Moran, as if convinced that she had misheard, pinched a wisp of hair away from an ear.

'May I ask the reason?' said Joe.

'Do I have to give a reason?'

'Not to me you don't.' Joe glanced at Carmel. 'But everybody in the Residents' Association isn't as broadminded as I am. People will want to know why you haven't signed and they'll expect an explanation from me. And they'll want to be sure that I put the case properly to you.'

'Oh, you can rest assured on that point; you have made your case clear,' Heinrich retorted. 'But surely you can understand that a person of my nationality…in my circumstances…has to be careful to avoid any action that could be misconstrued?'

'You've been here so long that we think of you as one of our own,' Joe lied smoothly.

At another time that remark might have flattered Heinrich, but by now he was exasperated at Joe, his annoyance heightened by the realisation that he couldn't spell out his reasons for declining to sign the petition because to do so would require a candour of which he was incapable. If he played his trump card he would, so to speak, have to explain how and where he had obtained it. He had always refused to wash German dirty linen in the presence of non-Germans.

'I want to get to bed early,' said Helen, buttoning her coat. 'I won't get much sleep for the rest of the week; they get their dole tomorrow.'

Joe reached for the plastic folder which he had propped against a chair-leg. He stood up.

'Give me that,' said Carmel. 'Have you a pen?'

Heinrich ached to squash the supercilious, triumphant, ripe apple that was Joe's face. Raspe's face had worn a similar look when Heinrich departed for the commandos. He had seen Raspe again, less than a year before, in a magazine photograph, in uniform. General Raspe, West German army and NATO, the caption said.

Heinrich managed an equable 'good night'. While Carmel was seeing Joe and Helen out, he hurried to the office where he gazed at the Victorian print in an attempt to revive the nostalgic, soothing sense of old world tranquillity that the picture usually created in him. The horse, whose head had been slightly angled towards the artist, had an air of nineteenth-century insouciance. Heinrich moved closer to the print. He had not noticed it before, but the horse was positively haughty.

The door flew open. Normally Carmel knocked before she entered the office.

'Don't you realise that we have to live with our neighbours?' she blazed, tugging at Heinrich's sleeve.

'Do you realise that you humiliated me?' he returned, shaking off her hand.

'It was the other way around. You hadn't the courage to tell me in advance that you weren't going to sign the thing.'

The door banged behind Carmel. She left him floundering, alone.

Chapter 10

Bill Sullivan sprawled on the leatherette sofa, laughing with Val and Bonny who, limpet-fashion, were attached to his work-scuffed boots. It was an evening ritual for them to help Daddy to take off his boots. He inhaled the aroma of liver and bacon which were frying in the closet-like back kitchen where Joan, eight months pregnant, was wedged between the gas cooker and sink. All day long Bill had been looking forward to dinner. It was Thursday, the day for lamb's liver, one of his favourite dishes. Val's bottom hit the linoleum as a boot came off suddenly in his hand. Bonny squealed her delight. Someone knocked on the front door. 'See who that is,' Joan called.

After kicking off the other boot, Bill, trailed by the children, padded in his stockinged-feet into the narrow hallway. He switched on the hall light and opened the door.

'Jim! Come in,' said Bill.

'God, it's cold,' said Jim Walsh, blowing into cupped hands. 'I won't keep you from your dinner. I'll be only a few minutes.'

The children and Bill trooped back to the living room. Jim followed. He knew the way: his own house, all the houses in Tuohy Place, were exactly the same design.

'It's really the kids I want to have a word with,' he said.

'Have they been up to some mischief?' Joan, entering from the back kitchen, asked anxiously.

'No,' Jim assured her. 'It's only that they were playing with my Shay today and he can't find his tricycle, and I thought that your kids might know where it is.'

Bonny and Val shook their blonde heads.

'I betcha anything *they* have it,' said Jim.

'You're probably right, Jim. You know I'd completely forgotten,' said Joan. She eased herself on to an arm of the sofa and perched there like an exotic bird in her billowy pale-pink smock.

'What did you forget? Who are you talking about?' demanded Bill.

Joan related how she had been shocked a few hours earlier to see two itinerant children romping with Val and Bonny and Shay Walsh. It was the luck of God that she had looked out the window when she did. She had rushed out, grabbed Val and Bonny, and pushed them indoors. She ordered Shay to go home and warned him that she would be telling his parents about him. And she had shouted at the itinerants to go away and stay with their own kind.

'You did the right thing,' said Jim to the rather breathless Joan. 'Shay told me that a couple of knackers were playing with him and your kids. Bold as brass, he was. I wasn't long about knocking the boldness out of him.'

Bill addressed Val and Bonny angrily: 'How many times have I told you not to mix with anyone from the camp?'

'But Daddy, we were playing,' said Bonny.

She and Val and Shay Walsh had stared at the children from the camp for ages and ages. And the children from the camp stared back at them. A little bit at a time, they all came closer and closer. Then everyone was talking. The children from the camp said their names were Davy and Ann.

Bonny wanted to touch Davy and Ann but Mammy and Daddy said the children from the camp were bold and they'd hurt you, and she was scared that touching them would be the same as when her hair got caught in a comb, or shampoo got into her eyes. Then Ann had touched her hand and Ann's hand was soft. And they were all touching, and she hugged Ann, who had earrings and a red ribbon. Ann and Davy weren't rough like Shay Walsh, who'd pinch you, and he said curses. Mammy and Daddy said the children from the camp were dirty, and when they said that, she thought of number two and creepy-crawly things like worms. Ann and Davy weren't dirty, no more dirty than she and Val and Shay were. All of them had mud on their hands and faces and clothes from tumbling on the grass, and they were all running and shouting and laughing.

'Pay attention when I'm talking to you!'

Why was Daddy so cross? He and Mammy and Mr Walsh were looking down at her and Val. Mammy and Mr Walsh were cross too. Val was starting to cry and so was she.

Bill, not wanting to appear soft in Jim Walsh's presence, refrained from comforting the weeping children. Instead he said, 'Stop that racket or I'll give you something to cry about.'

'Ah, don't mind them,' said Jim. 'My Shay's the same. He always kicks up a racket when he can't get his own way.'

Jim said goodbye to Joan and with a slight tilt of his head indicated his wish that Bill should follow him into the hallway.

'Bill, I didn't want to say too much in there in front of Joan but I'm not going to let those fucking knackers away with this. That tricycle cost me a nice few quid and I'm going up to the camp to get it back. Will you come with me?'

Jim, thin and wiry with fairish hair brushed back from his forehead, reminded Bill of a terrier on a hunt.

'Wouldn't it be better to call the guards?'

'Are you joking?' Jim exclaimed. 'What can they do?. They'd tell you themselves that their hands are tied by the law.'

Bill remembered his toolbox. He had reported its theft to the gardai, but he'd never seen the tools again. Still...going to the camp...you could lose your life up there. But Jim couldn't be allowed to go there on his own.

Another factor influenced Bill: his vice-chairmanship of the Residents' Association. He'd heard rumours that people in Tuohy Place were saying that he was getting above himself, that he was using his position in the association to hobnob with the likes of Joe Murphy. Bill dreaded anyone thinking he was an arselicker, and so he had severed contact with the Rugby Club, which had warmly welcomed him and where he had participated in and enjoyed two training sessions. He would have to show solidarity with Jim. He said, 'Give me a chance to have my dinner, then I'll go with you.'

'I'll call for you around half-seven,' said Jim.

Joe Murphy was turning away from the hallstand, where he had hung his coat and deposited his briefcase, when Jacqueline rushed towards him, clasped him, and buried her face in his stomach. She shook convulsively. Alarmed, he shoved her back gently.

'Daddy,' she sobbed.

Joe saw that even her lips were pale; the freckles on her nose were like currants in dough; her green eyes were red-rimmed.

'Jackie, my love,' he crooned. He carried her to the living room where he sat into an armchair with her on his lap. He kissed her wet, salty cheeks. He pressed his palms to her forehead, which to him felt unhealthily hot.

'Tell Daddy what's wrong.'

'She hit me.'

'Who? Your mother?'

'You're late this evening,' chided Sandra, coming through the archway from the kitchen. Joe, of course, hadn't bothered to telephone that he would be delayed, and she had to keep the dinner warm in the oven.

'Never mind about me,' said Joe. 'What have you done to Jacqueline?'

'Is she still snivelling?' Sandra said. Or neighed, thought Joe involuntarily. His wife neighed when she was excited or irritable. The neigh, together with the clipped accent she had acquired in an expensive convent boarding school, was a handy social weapon, a status symbol, that is when it was directed at others, not at him.

'Shouldn't the child be in bed?' he snorted. 'Look at her colour. She's obviously sick.'

'Whatever you say, doctor,' Sandra rejoined. She returned to the kitchen.

Jacqueline cuddled closer to Joe. 'My green jumper, the one with *Jackie* on the front, is all stained,' she whispered. 'You'll have to buy me a new jumper.'

'Of course Daddy will. But why is it stained. What happened?'

'From my nose. Oceans and oceans of blood came from my nose.'

Jacqueline explained how she had run to answer the doorbell because she wanted people to see her in her *Jackie* jumper and new lilac corduroy jeans. A horrid girl was outside, a girl from the camp. Jacqueline knew she was from the camp because she was dressed all sloppy. The girl struck her, struck her for nothing at all.

Joe lifted Jacqueline from his lap, jumped to his feet, and bellowed, 'This is intolerable. An innocent child attacked by one of those…those scum.'

Jackie. He slaved long hours, tolerated people he despised, paid huge insurance premiums, was robbed by taxes, was on the verge of ulcers, endured the vagaries of Irish weather when he should be holidaying abroad; but he didn't complain. It was all for her. The boys, his sons Pierce and Senan, he taught the value of money, showed them there was nothing for nothing, put them to work, cutting the lawn, weeding the garden, painting, watering the flowers, shifting furniture at auctions, helping him with the accounts. But he simply indulged Jacqueline. He had waited a long time for a daughter.

'What are you shouting about? Where are you going? I'm just about to serve dinner,' said Sandra, coming back into the living room.

'I'm going to the camp. I'll show those tinkers they're not dealing with my father now.'

'In heaven's name, don't be foolish, Joe,' Sandra pleaded. 'It was just a tiff between children.'

Jacqueline had a twinge of unease. Supposing the girl from the camp talked to Daddy? It wouldn't matter; he wouldn't believe the girl anyhow.

The front door banged behind Joe.

———————

'Jasus! Isn't that Murphy?' said Jim.

'It looks very like him,' Bill replied.

'I'll say one thing for Murphy: he's a cocky bastard,' said Jim, quickening his pace.

Dogs barked as he and Bill turned into the camp. Alerted by the tread of their boots on the hardened earth, Joe Murphy swivelled sharply and crouched defensively.

'Take it easy Joe. It's us,' said Bill, who noticed with relief that only one man and a woman were beside the fire. She fat, he thin, they lay mumbling against a log, bottles between them, looking incapable of any activity. Over near the fence were what appeared to be white dots, like mushrooms incandescent under a moon. A stick flamed on the fire and the dots became faces, children's faces. Bill counted three, but he couldn't be sure: the dots seemed to coalesce as the flame died.

Maggie McCarthy opened her eyes with difficulty. Shapes were wavering against the stars. The shapes were giving out. She wished they'd shut up and let her sleep.

A shade less fuddled than his wife, Tom McCarthy could discern three men and he believed he was talking to them, but for some reason that he couldn't fathom, they didn't appear to understand him. Only one man had been there at first, prancing around, shouting something about assault. Now another was shouting about a bicycle, or a tricycle, or something like that. The men were quality. He knew that by the way they talked.

'We're wasting our breath on these drunkards,' said Joe, frustrated. He had explained to Bill and Jim his reason for being at the camp. They, in turn, had told him about the missing tricycle. Now they looked at one another, at a loss to know what to do next.

Someone sneezed.

'Who's that?' said Joe.

'I think there's children over there,' Bill said.

'Hey you! Come over here,' Joe called.

'We can see you. It's no use trying to hide,' roared Jim.

Headlights swung in from the road, bobbed, and were switched off. An engine pinked out

'What's going on?' demanded Ned McCarthy, alighting from the van. He and Mikey Driscoll entered the circle of firelight.

Noel Fitzharris was pondering the unique warmth that was generated by physical exercise in frosty weather. Salubrious, that was the word to describe the warmth which, in his opinion, was one of life's best free gifts, infinitely preferable to the perspiration-producing heat of summer, and which, unlike the heat generated by fossil fuels, left the mind unclouded. The warmth ignited in the centre of one's body and diffused slowly to the extremities like—how would he term it?—like the sun spreading across a dawn sky.

Along River Road he walked, a reflective armband on the left sleeve of his overcoat, his pace lively, belying his sixty-six years. He saw the light from the camp-fire gradually brightening and the sound of voices drifted towards him.

Unbidden, the lines of a poem came to Noel as he neared the bend before the camp:

They are what their birth
And breeding suffer them to be;
Wild outcasts of society!

Who had written that? He was almost certain that it was Wordsworth, writing about gypsies. He'd been neglecting poetry lately; he'd make up for the omission, perhaps tonight. He rounded the bend and sighted the camp-fire. Further lines of the poem came back to him:

Men, women, children, yea the frame
Of the whole spectacle the same!
Only their fire seems bolder, yielding light,
Now deep and red, the colouring of night;
That on their Gypsy-faces falls…

He had no prior warning of the blow to his midriff. Winded, he staggered back and clawed at the air. The impact with the road jarred his spine. Footsteps hurried and the voices grew louder.

'It's Mr Fitzharris. Are you hurt?' Someone assisted him to his feet and handed him his hat. His spectacles were askew. He straightened them. He saw five men, one of whom he recognised as Joe Murphy. He heard a whimper. Its source was a child, a girl, lying on the road about a yard away.

Ned McCarthy stooped, gripped the girl's shoulders, and yanked her upwards. 'Did you hit this man's daughter?' he yelled.

Sheila McCarthy nodded an affirmative to her brother. 'But…' She didn't manage to say any more because Ned was shaking her. Shaking her so much that her teeth were rattling.

At the camp-fire, the man—he said his name was Murphy—had told Ned that his daughter was injured. Ned questioned her and Mary and Davy and Ann. At first she denied knowing anything about the man's daughter, but then she admitted that she was in River View Drive that day.

The door of the big bungalow was answered by a girl with golden hair flowing down her back. She was pretty. As pretty as a flower, Sheila thought. And she was wearing a lovely jumper and lovely jeans. The girl said, 'Go away, you filthy thing!' Sheila remembered once she had smelled a yellow flower and a wasp came out of the flower and stung her nose. She pulled up the flower and tore it to pieces. She hit the girl, punched her nose, and the girl wasn't pretty any more.

It would have been no use trying to explain all this to Mr Murphy because he was quality. And, Sheila reasoned, the quality could do anything they liked. Supposing he called the guards? She'd be sent to jail. The quality had pens and paper and, as far as she could gather, what they wrote was shocking important and could make your life easy or make it hard. And judges and nuns and priests were quality.

So she ran as fast as she could from the camp, until she ran into someone or something. Now Ned was shaking her. The pain! The pain in her ears. She was on the ground again and the men were towering over her.

Ned cuffed Sheila's ears not because he disapproved of her behaviour—he felt she'd probably been provoked—but because he believed that her attack on Murphy's daughter had given the settled community another stick with which to beat the travellers. And, ironically, he administered rough treatment because he wanted to protect his sister by preempting any retaliation by Murphy. Ned wouldn't countenance Murphy laying a finger on Sheila. Had he done so, he would have suffered violent consequences.

Ned was convinced that a traveller couldn't get justice from the quality, that the settled community would exaggerate even the smallest misdemeanour of a traveller into a major felony. He had bitter memories of his own court appearance. Six months he had got for hitting a guard and the judge had called him a ruffian. Another fellow, one of the quality, was also charged with assaulting the guard. A solicitor said the fellow was wild but that he came from a good family. The judge didn't call that fellow a ruffian and didn't send him to jail. He told him to behave himself and let him off with a fine.

Noel Fitzharris wished that he could console the crying girl who, like a discarded sack, lay crumpled on the road, but he was shy of children. Joe Murphy and Bill Sullivan didn't look at the girl, and avoided all eye-contact. 'I'm going home,' Bill said suddenly.

'What about the tricycle?' blustered Jim Walsh.

'Didn't you hear the childer saying that they didn't know notten about it?' replied Ned McCarthy. He lifted Sheila and, cradling her in his arms, he walked towards the camp-fire, accompanied by Mikey Driscoll.

Bill and Jim went home in Joe's Audi. Noel, though suffering the effects of his collision with the child, declined Joe's offer of a lift.

The next morning Jim spotted the tricycle behind the fuel shed in his back yard. He told Bill that the knackers had been frightened into returning it.

Chapter 11

A hen pheasant rose from a ditch, flew a few feet, then descended on a tuft of sedge. Quizzically, it eyed Heinrich and Eamonn. The shooting season wasn't long started and Heinrich surmised that the bird, which had probably been hand-reared by the gun club, was still semi-tame, associating humans with food, not with bullets.

Carmel had encouraged Heinrich and Eamonn to take a stroll while she was preparing dinner. They'd been to nine o'clock Mass. Both were in anoraks and their breaths condensed on the crystal air. High on their right was River Road, from which they could see smoke ascending.

'Senan Murphy told me his father was raging,' Eamonn said.

'Because I did not sign the petition?'

'Why didn't you sign?'

'Here, hold this down until I get over,' said Heinrich, indicating the top strand of the barbed-wire fence that separated the field from his garden. He scrambled over the fence. Eamonn vaulted it. They headed uphill towards the house.

'Would you have signed?' Heinrich countered.

Eamonn had no liking for the petition because he feared it might lead to Mary's departure from the area, or even worse, from Fernboro, but he couldn't reveal this to his father. As for the rest of the travellers, he didn't really know what to think: from an idealistic standpoint he

87

supposed that he should sympathise with them, though, on the other hand, he had to admit that they were a slovenly lot. Just look at their camp with its bottles and rags and tins and cartons. Most people hadn't a good word to say about them. Could everybody be wrong?

He'd read no books about the travellers, even presuming that such books existed, and he had come across no mention of them in history class at school. Television and radio referred to them occasionally, as did the newspapers, but he noticed that it always seemed to be a case of settled people pontificating about the travellers, just as people used to talk in front of their servants at one time as if the servants couldn't understand what was being said. Non-persons. That, Eamonn decided, was how the travellers were generally regarded.

'No, I don't think I would,' he replied. 'But you haven't told me why you refused to sign.'

'The petition may be harmless enough,' said Heinrich, pausing at the garden gate for a breather, 'but these things have a way of getting out of control.'

As had happened during the Nazi period, thought Eamonn. Matters had certainly got out of control then. Encouraged by his father's affability, he ventured, 'I have been thinking about something you said, when you were in my room, about not needing pictures to tell you what happened. What did you mean by that?'

'You seem to have concluded that I meant something particular.'

'Well, it was the way you said it...that's what struck me when I thought about it afterwards.'

'Ah, chaps! There you are. Carmel posted you missing.' Philip Shaw came into view, beaming at Heinrich and Eamonn from underneath the deerstalker that he invariably resurrected for the shooting season. Carmel had invited Philip to dinner.

Across the river a shotgun blasted and birds, mainly pigeons, wheeled in noisy alarm over the trees.

––––––––––

Heinrich didn't need pictures to tell him what had happened, but with each passing year he found the enormity of what had happened more difficult to believe.

Entertainment for the Troops
Venue: North-west of Odessa
Date: Mid-September 1941
Admission: Free
Cast: 1,000, more or less
Genre: Roman Colosseum realism
Dramatis Personae: Superhumans, Subhumans
Producer: Adolf Hitler
Assistant Producers: Heinrich Himmler and a host of others
Created by: Collaborative. Input from Roman Catholicism, Russian Orthodoxy, Protestantism, Statesmen, Intellectuals, Artists, National Socialism
Theme: Control of vermin (hitherto called heretics and Christ-killers)
Choreography: Unpredictable because unrehearsed
Lighting: The sun
Costumes: Superfluous
Scenery: Naturalistic
Director: Heinrich Obermeyer

Act I
Scene I
Northern side of railway embankment. At base of embankment is a pit. At eastern end of pit and at right angles to the embankment is a large pile of earth. Opposite the pile of earth and on the embankment soldiers lounge. Bottles of vodka and schnapps pass from hand to hand. Many soldiers are smoking cigarettes. Some are in bathing trunks. The sun is hot. Seated at a corner of the pit with his legs dangling into it is a shirt-sleeved corporal. An automatic pistol rests on his knees.
Schnell! Schnell!
Corporal (picking up pistol and grinning at the soldiers): Pay attention, lads, the show is about to begin.
About twenty people, men, women, children, file from behind the pile of earth. A sergeant, ten privates, and Lieutenant Obermeyer escort them. The sergeant indicates to the people that they should descend steps that are cut into the side of the pit. Down the steps the people go, the agile assisting the elderly. A baby, sleeping, is passed from person to person. Leica cameras held by several soldiers reflect the sun.

First Soldier (pointing towards pit): Look at her!

Second Soldier: Where? Where? Oh…it's a pity to waste her.

The girl holds her head high. She stares straight ahead. She retains her balance on the steps by touching the pit wall with her left hand. She reaches the pit floor. She places her left arm across her breasts. Her right hand shields her vulva. She wears no clothes. All the people in the pit are naked.

Sergeant: Fall in!

The privates and corporal line up on the side of the pit facing the embankment. Each private has a magazine rifle.

Sergeant (bending his knees and pointing to the ground): Kneel down!

The people in the pit kneel. A man, perhaps its father, clasps the baby to his chest.

Sergeant: *Obersturmführer*, shall we begin?

Lieutenant Obermeyer (cap tilted forward, peak hiding his eyes): Yes, *Unterscharführer*.

Scene II

Railway embankment. Truck. On its bonnet is an officer's cap. Beside the truck is Lieutenant Obermeyer. He crouches. He retches. Sergeant approaches.

Sergeant (kindly): This is your first action, sir?

Lieutenant Obermeyer removes handkerchief from trousers pocket. Using handkerchief, he mops his forehead, wipes his mouth, blows his nose. Sergeant proffers bottle of vodka. Lieutenant Obermeyer gulps from bottle.

Scene III

Pit (hours later).

First Soldier: This is boring—just the same thing over and over again. I'm going.

Second Soldier: At least we'll have a few good pictures—I've used all my film.

(Exit First Soldier and Second Soldier).

About twenty people, men, women, children, file from behind the pile of earth. A Sergeant, ten Privates, and Lieutenant Obermeyer escort them. Some of the privates sway. Lieutenant Obermeyer's eyes are glazed. Out of the pit, where they have spread a thin layer of soil, climb four civilians, peasants. They haven't far to climb. The pit is nearly full. Its sides and edges are spattered red. So are the corporal's shirt, trousers, boots, arms and hands. He lights one cigarette off another. (The smoke deadens the smell. Fear produces various effects. Some urinate, some excrete, some vomit, some sweat, some weep, some salivate. Some do all six. Some do two or more. Some don't appear to do any of the six. All bleed). Flies buzz. The people are in the pit. They tread gingerly. (They don't want to step on faces).

Sergeant (bending his knees and pointing to the ground): Kneel down!

The people in the pit kneel. The sergeant looks at Lieutenant Obermeyer. Lieutenant Obermeyer nods.

Sergeant: Aim. Fire!

Crows stay rooted to the railway line. (They have grown accustomed to the shooting). Moans come from the pit. A grey-bearded man, hands on stomach, writhes.

Lieutenant Obermeyer (shouting): You clumsy fools.

Sergeant: The men are exhausted, sir. They are inclined to aim low so as not to miss the children. *Rottenführer!*

The corporal steps into the pit. He wades through bodies. He points the automatic pistol at the grey-bearded man's temple. He pulls the trigger.

(Enter *Wehrmacht* Captain).

Captain (gesturing at soldiers): Get out of here! At once! That's an order!

(Soldiers begin to exit).

The Captain stands at edge of pit. Stares at Lieutenant Obermeyer. The Captain's expression is disdainful.

Captain (indicating pit): You haven't even the decency to arrange the bodies in an orderly fashion.

Act II
Scene I
Railway embankment (early next morning). Peasants topping up pit.

Peasant (brandishing shovel): Clear off, you brutes.

Dogs retreat. Crows have resumed their station on the railway line.

(Enter Lieutenant Obermeyer)

Rusty-red trail leads from north-western corner of pit. Lieutenant Obermeyer follows the trail. He reaches hedge.

(Exit Lieutenant Obermeyer)

Scene II

Western side of hedge. Woman's body. Naked. Legs apart. Corporal kneeling beside body.

Lieutenant Obermeyer (angrily): You animal!

Corporal (rises to feet; salutes sluggishly): This one must have crawled from the pit during the night, but as you can see, sir, she didn't get far.

Lieutenant Obermeyer: That doesn't excuse your disgusting behaviour.

Corporal (rubbing right hand on trousers): It's not what you think, sir. You wouldn't believe where these people conceal valuables. The *Standartenführer* has instructed us to search everywhere. Of course, if I'd found anything, I would have handed it over to you (Corporal's tone becomes insinuating) and you would give it to the proper authorities.

Lieutenant Obermeyer: Yes, I would. Now get someone to help you bury this body.

Scene III

Railway embankment (later same morning). Sonderkommandos load two trucks with clothing and footwear (which is destined for the NSV, the National Socialist relief organisation. Charitable ladies will distribute the goods to the needy. Watches are kept separate. They go to the forces at the front).

Sergeant (addressing Lieutenant Obermeyer): Look at those vultures.

Peasant women hover nearby. Some women stand on a mound. (Under the mound are the owners of the clothing, footwear, and watches).

A commando prances about. He holds a long-legged knickers to his waist. (Laughter).

Lieutenant Obermeyer's features relax. He grins. He laughs. And laughs.

Curtain.

There were many repeat performances, thought Heinrich, splashing cold water on his face. After towelling his face, he left the bathroom, descended the stairs, and entered the dining room. Appetising aromas drifted from the kitchen. On the sideboard was a decanter from which Heinrich pulled the stopper.

'How about you, Philip?' he asked, holding up the decanter.

'No, thank you, old man, I have sufficient for the moment,' said Philip, who was in a fireside armchair. He resumed his conversation with Eamonn who, glass of Coke in hand, was standing beside the fire.

In one gulp Heinrich swallowed a generous measure of brandy. He refilled his glass.

Carmel, entering from the kitchen, frowned. She'd noticed that Heinrich's drinking had increased lately. He was actually tipsy the previous Wednesday night after their altercation over the petition.

At the table Carmel sat facing Heinrich. Philip was on her right, opposite Eamonn.

'I'll have them soon. The pheasants, you know,' said Philip, forking Yorkshire pudding.

Carmel assumed a smile. Though she would never reveal it to him, she detested the pong of hanging pheasants, and it was only by a supreme effort that she could bring herself to prepare and cook them. But Philip ritually supplied her with the birds two or three times a year.

'Why don't you chaps come out to Fern Park?' Philip continued. 'Donoghue won't miss a few brace.'

'Eamonn can go with you,' said Heinrich, lifting a wine glass. 'As you know, fishing is more in my line.'

'Is that acceptable to you, Eamonn?' Philip enquired eagerly.

'Of course. It'll be great.'

'Splendid. We'll have a topping time. The dogs are in fine shape.'

Philip and Eamonn animatedly discussed plans for their shooting expedition. As often before, Philip's accent reminded Heinrich of the colonel in the prisoner-of-war camp. Heinrich, by then a captain, surrendered to the British in April, 1945. In September 1942, through the powerful contacts of his uncle Walter, he had been reinstated in the *Wehrmacht* after a year in the *Sonderkommandos*. Then he had served in Italy, whence he had been transferred to France shortly before the Normandy invasion.

'I see there's a bit of a hullabaloo building up over the camp,' said Philip, stirring his coffee.

Carmel resumed her seat after clearing the dessert plates. She looked quickly at Heinrich; by unspoken agreement, they had since Wednesday night avoided discussing anything pertaining to the petition. She said: 'It's the politicians and the newspapers. They're blowing it out of proportion.'

'I believe there is some sort of petition,' said Philip.

'Mother has signed it. Father hasn't,' chirped Eamonn.

'Oh, I say, I didn't mean to...'

'Who do you think is correct, Father or Mother?'

'Eamonn!' said Carmel.

'I think it is a fair question. I should like to hear what you have to say, Philip,' Heinrich said. He was still visualising the colonel whose typical English superciliousness—that was how he had regarded it—he had yearned to deflate. But it would have been extremely hazardous to draw attention to himself; supposing the colonel had learned of the gap in his *Wehrmacht* career?

'About the petition, you mean?' said Philip.

'Yes.'

'Well, Heinrich, you know...for me it's rather a hypothetical question.'

'What about your Protestantism which, according to you, expects a man to think for himself?' Heinrich was smiling but his tone was tinged with harshness.

Carmel protested, 'I don't think you are being quite fair to Philip ...'
Heinrich said, 'Let him answer.'

'I was talking about Protestantism from a general viewpoint, from the viewpoint of belief, if you like,' said Philip.

'But surely action or inaction, such as signing or not signing a petition, is governed by belief?' Eamonn said.

'Not always,' replied Philip. 'In the army, for instance—and I'm sure your father had much the same experience—one sometimes does things of which one doesn't necessarily approve or believe in.'

Heinrich looked sharply at Philip.

'We're still waiting for your opinion on the petition,' Eamonn persisted.

'I tell you what; I'll have a word with higher authority first.'

'Higher authority?' queried Eamonn.

'Yes, the Padre, the Protestant Minister, you know.'

Chapter 12

A wit said it was the first time within living memory that there was silence at the back of the church during Sunday Mass. The silence didn't endure throughout the whole of last Mass in St Bridget's Church on that third Sunday in November: it coincided with Fr James Kearney's sermon. And, frankly, the back of the church wasn't totally silent—it was just less noisy than usual.

The congregation's interest was aroused even before the sermon began. Fr Kearney removed his outer vestment, a green chasuble, handed it to an altar boy, proceeded to the marble communion rail, entered the Epistle aisle through a brass gate, continued for a few yards, and ascended the pulpit. People surmised that he was going to say something important: the pulpit had seldom been used in recent years. It had the forlorn aspect of a stage without a player, merely an ornament, however striking, of sculpted white marble. Priests had grown accustomed to delivering their homilies from a tall lectern in the sanctuary.

Fr Kearney tested the microphone by tapping it with his right forefinger; loudspeakers throughout the church responded. He pulled up the lace-trimmed sleeves of the alb that was too large for him, opened the ledger in which were inscribed the weekly notices and extracted from it the text of his sermon. A note in the ledger caught his eye. The note, in Canon Ryan's handwriting, castigated those who remained at or outside the church doors during Mass. Fr Kearney decided to say nothing about the matter, for he feared that such castigation might lead to some of the culprits staying away altogether.

Mary McCarthy wasn't one of the culprits: she was inside the doors, not very far inside, on a bench parallel to the wall of the Gospel aisle. From where she sat, Fr Kearney seemed to be a long way off, just a head on a higher level than all the other heads. Arms folded across a salmon-pink jumper, she basked in the warmth that came from a radiator behind the bench. This was her favourite part of the Mass, when the priest talked and talked and she sat back and let her mind wander. She didn't attend Mass every Sunday, hardly ever in the summer, and she didn't realise that it was sinful not to attend. To her religion meant saying prayers to Jesus and his Blessed Mother; it meant nuns and priests. You had to have a priest to christen you, to give you Communion, to marry you, to bless you when you were dying, to bury you. Nuns were holy, and because they were holy they were nice to you—well, most of them were. Then there were Protestants. She knew nothing about them except that many of them were rich and a lot of them were decent, but because they were Protestants they couldn't go to heaven.

At the end of a seat across the aisle from Mary was Noel Fitzharris. Though she didn't know his name, she recognised him as the man Sheila had run into at the camp that night over a week before. The next day he had called to the camp with a bag of sweets and money for Sheila, and after asking her how she was, had rushed away.

Fr Kearney read the notices, then smoothed the writing-pad sheets which contained his sermon. 'My dear people,' he began. He paused and waited for the coughing to cease or at least to lessen.

'In today's Gospel, Jesus tells us that the kingdom of heaven is like a grain of mustard seed.' Fr Kearney's voice had a pleasant, varied pitch. 'The seed becomes a tree and the birds come and dwell in its branches. Has such a tree taken root in our parish? Regretfully, I have to say that in Fernboro the seed has apparently fallen on barren soil.'

Upturned faces eyed the pulpit. Ah, they're listening, thought Fr Kearney. He went on, 'Our parish is a barren, inhospitable and hostile place for certain human beings. I am referring to our neighbours on

River Road, the itinerants.'

Itinerants. The word gusted from the loudspeaker in the porch, like an east wind. 'Did you hear that?' said Bill Sullivan, interrupting Jim Walsh's spinning of a smutty yarn. They were leaning against the open main door of the church.

Silence fell on the crowd that was spilling from the porch on to the tarmacadamed forecourt.

'For itinerants there is no mustard tree in Fernboro, no branches shelter them,' Fr Kearney continued. 'Because the seed has not germinated, they are at the mercy of the elements. We have not nurtured the seed; we have excluded itinerants from our Christian love which should encompass all our neighbours. Our Christianity, so to speak, rests on the topsoil: it has not taken root.'

Helen Moran tightened the knot on her headscarf. She believed that women and girls should cover their heads in church, a practice that was disappearing rapidly. She was seated at an angle to the pulpit, eleven or twelve yards away. She was incensed. She came to Mass to worship God, to forget the cares of the world, not to hear about tinkers. Love your neighbour indeed! It would be more in Fr Kearney's line to go up to the camp and tell the tinkers how to love their neighbours. But he's young, full of new ideas. Nonsense, a lot of them. Canon Ryan should have a talk with him.

'My dear people, remember the words of Jesus: "Judge nobody and you will not be judged; condemn nobody and you will not be condemned; forgive and you will be forgiven." Is that how we treat our neighbours, the itinerants? Do we not judge them by our own standards? Do we not condemn them because they are unlike the rest of us? Do we ever forgive them, that is, supposing that there is something to forgive? Do we ever think how impossible it is for them to be like the rest of us when they can't even send their children to school because we won't permit them to remain in the one place long enough?'

Mary McCarthy became aware that she was the centre of surreptitious glances, sneaky looks, in her vocabulary. She checked her jumper, skirt, and shoes. They were, so far as she could see, in order. And she had washed her face and combed her hair that morning.

'Itinerants are also the responsibility of our public representatives...'

The priest is talking about us, Mary realised, surprised and discomfited. I suppose he's giving out about us. That must be why they're looking at me. No matter what you wear or where you are they always know that you're a traveller.

'But if one is to believe the newspapers, they are not shouldering that responsibility,' Fr Kearney was saying. 'It appears—and I say this with deep reluctance—that our public representatives are more concerned with political survival and advancement than with justice.'

Councillor Liam Lehane bristled. Here, he thought, is a blatant example of pulpit politics—a priest interfering in something that is none of his damn business. Didn't we suffer enough in the past from such carry-on? In a sky-blue anorak, Councillor Lehane stood at a pillar near the top of the Gospel aisle. Apart from annoyance at Fr Kearney's remarks, he was in high spirits. On the previous Wednesday night a deputation from River Road Residents' Association had presented a petition to a special meeting of the Town Council and he had formally introduced the deputation. That was mud in the eye of Councillor Dooley, the snobbish bastard.

Councillor Lehane was sure that most of the votes of River Road would come to him—and there'd be a lot more elsewhere. Look at all the publicity he was getting. Even the Hitler remark seemed to have done him good: people shook his hand and congratulated him on having had the courage to say what he thought. Now he was even feeling rather benign towards itinerants: without them he'd still be searching for an issue, still be stuck on the lower rungs of the ladder.

Fr Kearney was again quoting Jesus: '"Love your enemies; do good to those who hate you; bless those who curse you; pray for those who treat you insultingly." By no stretch of the imagination can itinerants be classified as our enemies. Yet they are denied not only Christian love, but they also are often deprived of basic human respect. "As you would have men treat you, you are to treat them." That is what Jesus says. My dear people, let us nourish the seed; let the tree grow in Fernboro. In the name of the Father and of the Son and of the Holy Spirit.'

Carrying the ledger, Fr Kearney descended the pulpit steps. The Church rang with coins as wooden bowls were passed from hand to hand and from seat to seat.

Ted Corkery went into action. Passing through the sanctuary, he entered the sacristy where, with other collectors, he emptied the bowls and began sorting and counting coins. Notes were easily counted; they were few in number. Ted wasn't particularly religious but it was expedient that a building contractor should maintain good relations with the clergy, who often had valuable contracts at their disposal. The fact that Nuala, his daughter, was a nun was also an asset.

He was feeling vaguely uneasy. That morning he'd had a call from TJ Fennell, the Town Engineer, who said he wanted to discuss something important, but not over the phone. Something to do with itinerants, Fennell had said.

Noel Fitzharris was mentally applauding Fr Kearney on his sermon, and resolved to meet the priest, with whom he already had a slight acquaintance.

'Bullshit,' was Jim Walsh's comment on the sermon. He resumed his spinning of smutty yarns.

Bill Sullivan was pondering Fr Kearney's words. He decided that Fr Kearney didn't understand the situation. The itinerants would be better off if they had to leave River Road because the Town Council or County Council would probably have to find them a proper camp-site. So, Bill concluded, River Road residents were really doing the itinerants a favour.

A bell tinkled through the loudspeaker, signalling the Consecration. Bill brightened. Once the Consecration was over, he and Jim would slip away to the pub, to Gradys.

———

'We don't want to jeopardise the Fern Heights scheme,' said TJ Fennell to Ted Corkery, slowly exhaling cigarette smoke through his small nose and wide mouth. His head was tonsured, his skin leathery and lined. His drooping eyelids, drawling voice, and deliberate movements created an impression of languor. But he was always on the alert, like a lizard for flies.

'There's surely no danger of that?' said Ted Corkery, alarmed. They were in the living room of TJ's bungalow.

It was Ted who had erected the bungalow. That was four years ago, and he'd made no profit on the job, regarding it as an investment in TJ's goodwill.

Colonnaded, with cream walls and red-tiled roof, the bungalow really belonged to a sunny clime. Nevertheless, the house was greatly admired by many people. 'Grand' was the word most often used to describe it. It was in a secluded spot, up a specially constructed avenue off the Loop Road. TJ had taken advantage of the seclusion by diverting Council workers and machinery from their normal duties and engaging them in clearing the site, digging foundations, excavating for a septic tank, transporting and spreading topsoil, seeding the lawn. Dolefully aware that they would splash the money on beer, he had paid the workers twenty pounds a man out of his own pocket to ensure they would keep their mouths shut.

'There's every danger of it if the racket over the itinerants doesn't die down,' replied TJ. 'And, as you know, Dooley has been asking questions about Fern Heights. It's lucky for us that he's not very bright, though he is a solicitor.'

Ted, with other investors, had purchased three acres at Fern Heights, on the northern side of town. He was confident of squeezing up to twenty houses into the site. TJ had facilitated planning permission and prepared designs for the scheme.

'Dooley doesn't have to be bright; he inherited his practice,' said Ted. 'Anyway, I don't think we need worry about Councillor Dooley. He's only a politician and I know a way of quietening him down.'

TJ lit another cigarette. 'That may be so, but I have to cover my own tracks. Councillors had forgotten about the River Road bend until the racket started about the itinerants. What we have to do at this stage is to ensure that the itinerants remain where they are, because their presence is an excuse for not working on the bend. But if they go, I may have to stop work on the road at Fern Heights and use the remainder of the funds to make a start on removing the bend.'

Ted did rapid calculations: it was essential that he should begin the Fern Heights scheme in the spring; otherwise, bank interest would eat away at his profits. But he couldn't begin without the road, which was essential for machinery and the transport of building materials. He asked, 'What do you suggest?'

You'll have to fill the role of peacemaker,' said TJ, with a dry laugh. 'You know the kind of thing: speak quietly to people, flatter them. Be a calming influence on the Residents' Association.'

'That's very easy to say but how am I supposed to calm the likes of Joe Murphy? And what about Councillor Lehane?'

'Lehane is just playing politics. Most people realise that,' TJ said. 'As for Murphy, try to isolate him. He can't do very much once the Residents' Association is more or less neutralised. All we have to do is to play for time. The itinerants will eventually move of their own accord and we'll be into a new financial year, which means that the Council can vote another sum to remove the River Road bend. We'll be in the clear then.'

Ted Corkery glumly agreed to do his best.

Chapter 13

The throb of rock music ebbed and flowed with the swinging to and fro of the inner door through which teenagers tripped to the dance. Incessant drumbeats and snarling, sobbing guitars electrically charged Mary McCarthy, who was swaying rhythmically, impatient to plunge into the gyrating throng. With each swing of the door she caught a glimpse of the dancers: twisting, turning, jumping, jiving figures, speckled under dim multi-coloured light.

She was in the foyer of the parish hall, accompanied by Ned and Bridgie and Lukey and his fiancée, Thrush Stokes. Lukey, who had said he would pay for them all, was at the head of the queue now, bending towards the hatch in the ticket office, tendering a five-pound note. He straightened and came away from the office. His right hand was extended, the fiver between thumb and forefinger.

'They won't let us in,' said Lukey. Thrush, a natural blonde who was around the same age as Mary, touched his arm. Lukey avoided looking at Thrush. His eyes were downcast, following the progress of a wood-louse across the floor. A boy in the queue stomped, leaving a minuscule stain on a buff tile.

'Do you not have enough money?' asked Mary, who had stopped swaying.

'Of course I have,' Lukey replied.

'Well, what's wrong then? Why can't we get in?' Ned demanded.

'You know…they don't want us here,' said Lukey softly. He was acutely conscious of the people in the queue and of the man collecting tickets at the inner door.

'Give me that!' said Ned, snapping the fiver. Ignoring the queue, he went to the hatch. 'I want five tickets, please.'

'I'm sorry. As I told your friend, we can't let you in,' said Joe Murphy from behind the hatch. Neither he nor Ned gave any hint of mutual recognition.

'We just want to have a dance.'

'Next please!'

Ned felt a tap on his left shoulder. 'Could I have a word with you?' said Ted Corkery cordially. Apart from collecting tickets, it was his task to anticipate and to prevent trouble.

Reluctantly, Ned left the hatch, and preceded by Ted, rejoined his companions. Ted smiled on them all. He said, 'I hope you will accept my apology, but you see this is a dance for the youth…'

'Aren't we young?' queried Bridgie caustically.

'Yes, but I was about to say that the dance is for the youth club. You can't attend if you're not a member of the club, or unless you've been invited.'

'How do you join?' said Ned.

Ted thought rapidly. 'You have to fill in a form. I'm afraid it involves a lot of writing.' Scanning the dejected faces, he congratulated himself on his inspiration; tinkers hated anything to do with forms or writing.

Thrush clasped Lukey's hand. Wordlessly, they left the hall. After a few hesitant seconds, Mary and Ned and Bridgie followed.

Ted stood outside the entrance door, to make sure that they left. 'I'm sorry about this,' he called after them. And, indeed, he was a bit sorry, principally for the girls—particularly the little pretty, dark-haired one. He went back in.

'I've got to hand it to you, Corkery; you know how to deal with them,' chuckled Joe, who was stretching his legs in the foyer after his cramped stint in the ticket office. It was ten o'clock and the rush was over; the dance would end at midnight.

Joe and Ted were on the parents' committee of the youth club, and tonight it was their turn to supervise the dance. Their duties, totally voluntary, were mainly concerned with the morals of the dancers: absolutely banned were petting and alcohol and prolonged mouth-kissing, cuddling was frowned upon, and girls were expected to dress modestly. There were no written guidelines on these matters, so each adult supervisor had to make impromptu decisions. The decisions didn't always tally, which meant that some supervisors were more popular than others with the dancers. Though it gave most of them headaches, the supervisors favoured rock music: it wasn't conducive to close dancing.

The youth club, whose nominal president was the parish priest, Canon Ryan, had been founded six years previously with the avowed aim of catering for all classes in and around Fernboro, and in particular for what was termed 'disadvantaged youth'. But most members were secondary school students; those who had left school at primary level and who were in dead-end jobs or unemployed seldom came near the club. There was also a tacit understanding that all members should be Roman Catholics. Clergy on both sides, and probably a majority of the laity, agreed that adolescence was an inappropriate time to bring Catholics and Protestants together, given the churches' conflicting views on mixed marriages.

The club's weekly dances were, parents hoped, a counter-attraction to Fernboro's commercial ballroom and the insidious new lounge bars into which ballad and music sessions were enticing a growing number of teenagers.

'Still, I suppose, it wouldn't have done any great harm to let them in,' said Ted.

'What!' exclaimed Joe. 'And have our kids dancing with tinkers and maybe even walking home with them. That would destroy the whole purpose of our petition.'

Ted didn't reply. Mention of the petition had reminded him of his recent conversation with TJ Fennell, the Town Engineer.

Mary, her brothers, and Bridgie and Thrush dawdled along Chapel Street, within earshot of the rock music thumping through the asbestos-sheeted roof of the parish hall. Into the tinselled, crèpe-papered Christmas windows the girls peered, at clothes, jewellery, toys, cosmetics and chocolate-box pictures.

'We'll have chips,' Ned decreed.

They quickened their pace, glad to have somewhere to go. It was too late for the cinema, too early to return to the camp. Appetising aromas wafted out to them as they neared Dino's, which had a neon sign that blazed like a beacon on the southern side of the Town Square. At the orange formica-topped take-away counter, Ned ordered five bags of chips, amply sprinkled with vinegar, and five bunburgers, doused in tomato ketchup. Lukey paid the bill.

Eating as they went, they came back into High Street. Mary bit into her bunburger, ketchup dripping from the corners of her mouth and trickling down her chin. Quickly she stemmed the flow with a hand-kerchief. It wouldn't do for the sauce to drip on to the collar of her blouse. Pale green the blouse was, or rather, the shirt. It had belonged to him. To Eamonn. She had learned his name from his mother.

She'd been thinking of him while she prepared for the dance. She shampooed her hair outdoors. Then she managed to get her parents' caravan to herself and she locked the door. Alternately kneeling and standing in a large plastic basin, the baby's bath, she washed from head to toe with scented soap. She was ages using eyeshadow and scent and lipstick and nail varnish that she had borrowed from Bridgie.

She picked up the shirt, which had lain neatly folded on a bunk, and buried her face in it, inhaling its machine-washed cleanliness. Eamonn's mother, saying that he had outgrown it, had given her the shirt a week or so ago, and she had hoarded it in a plastic bag under her pillow. She kissed the shirt, unfolded it, and started to put it on, savouring the caress of the soft fabric on her arms, her shoulders, her neck. Folding her arms across her breasts, she hugged herself. Eamonn was holding her and they were dancing.

She saw him most days: she knew the times when he came and went to school. Usually he was with others, often girls in their stupid convent uniforms. She stayed in the background, fearing, yet hoping, that he would notice her. One day they had met unexpectedly, around a corner, and he had said hello and was gone before she could reply.

He would understand her: he must know about things because he was still going to school and was always carrying books. They'd hold hands, and he'd listen to her. He wouldn't make a laugh of her, wouldn't mind about her being a traveller. Oh, God! please let him be at the dance.

She buttoned the shirt and tucked it into her blue denim jeans. Then she put on the round-necked, salmon-pink jumper that she had rinsed out the previous day. She emerged from the caravan and emptied the basin. Not wanting to smell of wood smoke, she avoided the camp-fire. She sat into her father's van, switched on the interior light, adjusted the rear-view mirror, and gave her face a final scrutiny.

Ned crumpled an empty chip bag and flung it into the gutter. From a shop doorway in Wolfe Tone Street, the young people could again hear the muffled beat of music from the parish hall.

'I wish we could sit down somewhere,' said Bridgie. Mary agreed. Her energy seemed to have drained away. The music from the hall, the Christmas lights, the bright shop windows, the sound of revellery from the pubs—all depressed her, and in her sight were Thrush and Lukey, she with an arm around his waist, he with an arm around her shoulders.

'Ye know what?' said Ned. 'Ye girls could probably get into the dance if me and Lukey weren't with ye.'

'Ah, it's too late now,' Bridgie said.

'No, no, it's not,' interjected Mary. 'They're just beginning to come out of the pubs. It's only around eleven o'clock.'

'Girls, ye go on ahead,' said Ned, 'and me and Lukey'll come on behind.'

With money from Lukey in their hands, the girls, Mary in the lead, retraced their steps towards the parish hall. When they had turned into Chapel Street, Ned and Lukey began to follow them.

The more he brooded on what had happened in the hall, the more annoyed Ned became. On the surface, at least, they had been treated like human beings. They'd been furnished with a seemingly valid reason for being refused entry to the dance, and had even received an apology. But now he was convinced that they'd been outwitted. They had been turned away for one reason only, the same reason as always. He wouldn't have minded so much if the girls hadn't been there. He shouldn't have left the hall so quietly and easily but if he hadn't done so, the guards might have been called and he might have ended up in court. He might have ended up in jail again.

'We'll wait here a while,' he said, leaning against the bars of the high railing that enclosed St Bridget's Church. He and Lukey could see but couldn't hear the girls, who were gesticulating in a patch of light in front of the hall. Bridgie, who was the tallest, seemed to push Mary against the door.

Mary stumbled to a halt in the foyer. Bridgie and Thrush tiptoed in behind her. They glanced through the grille of the ticket office. The booth was unoccupied. They giggled. Music rocked. Mary pointed towards the inner door. Bridgie and Thrush nodded.

One step was all that Mary managed to take into the cavernous, pulsating interior. A whiff of body-heated air, a flash of starry lights, then she found herself back in the foyer.

'Oh no, you don't!' cried Joe Murphy, releasing his hold on her shoulder. He had been just inside the inner door, keeping a moral eye on the dancers.

Arms outspread, he advanced on the girls. 'Out! Out!' he piped. His left hand accidentally brushed Bridgie's chest.

'Listen Mister, we're not hens,' she shouted, standing her ground, bosom thrust forward in tight white jumper, chin down, legs elongated in bell-bottom red slacks. Her voice seemed unnaturally loud in the sudden silence; the four members of the rock group had paused to mop sopping brows and gulp soft drinks. Apparently encouraged by the sound of her own voice, Bridgie worked herself into a paroxysm. Waving a fist in Joe's face, she screeched, 'You're notten but a dirty old man. You fuckin' sex maniac. We're not good enough for your fuckin' dance but you wouldn't mind ridin' us!'

Bridgie's audience was growing. People, wondering what the racket was about, were pouring into the foyer.

'He assaulted me. He had a feel when no one was watching.' Her speech fragmented into hysterical sobs.

'Why you...' Joe, white-faced, also lapsed into incoherence.

'It's OK, Joe, I'll handle this,' said Ted Corkery, emerging from the crowd.

Mary and Thrush tried to calm Bridgie. Mary looked at the gaping adolescent audience, physically so near, yet of a different world. 'Fuck ye!' she hissed. Then her eyes met Eamonn's.

Hair dark and limp with sweat, shirt open and clinging to his chest, exposing silver cross and chain, Eamonn had been standing stockstill, overcome by a sweet-sad longing as he gazed at Mary, seeing her for the first time in lingering close-up. Then she uttered the expletive. He wouldn't have been more surprised if a swallow had cawed like a jackdaw.

A swallow: graceful, elusive, migratory.

It was as if she were of a separate species from him. He wished that she were not an itinerant, yet, somehow, the fact that she was added to her attractiveness. He craved to meet her, yet when he saw her approaching he crossed to the other side of a street or road. And he frequently and unnecessarily passed the camp-site, walking fast, darting glances, yet trying to appear nonchalant.

In his imagination he often hugged and kissed her, never proceeding further; she was inviolate. He had numerous imaginary conversations with her, always lovingly harmonious.

He was a hero in his fancy: diving from the town bridge, rescuing her from a flood-swollen Fern, kissing her back to life, she in a hospital bed flinging her arms around his neck; or he was snatching her from the path of a careering car, tumbling with her within inches of dizzily spinning wheels; he, injured, bandaged, stoical; in hospital, she visiting him, flinging arms around him.

His eyes. Mary was oblivious of everyone and everything else. Then the music restarted. Eamonn averted his gaze. People began to drift back to the dance. 'Come on, girls,' said Ted Corkery.

'Please, sir, can't you let us stay on?' said Mary. 'We'll pay. We have the money.'

'You know well it's not a question of money.'

Bridgie, now listless, and Thrush walked towards the entrance door. Mary looked at Eamonn. He didn't return the look. She followed Bridgie and Thrush.

Eamonn watched Mary's retreat. At the door she turned and their eyes met again. Hers, under long lashes, seemed to him to be liquid, and he understood the message from their moist depths. Just a few paces... He strained against the shackles but, inhibited by the presence of others, especially that of his friends Senan Murphy and Cathal Corkery, he stayed where he was. On his side of the barrier.

'There's no point in taking chances,' said Ted Corkery, bolting the door.

'By God, that big blondy bitch is a real tinker,' said Joe Murphy. He was holding a bottle of lemonade and colour had returned to his cheeks. 'I have a good mind to get her arrested for character assassination.'

The entrance door rattled violently against the bolt. 'Come out, ye fuckin' bastards!'

Ned McCarthy hurled himself against the door. He bounced off it. He kicked the door. Kicked and kicked, and shouted, till he tired.

Mary, in the tent that night, ripped off the shirt, scattering buttons.

Chapter 14

The bleating of a goat awoke Joe Murphy on the morning of Thursday, 7 December. Some hours later, Helen Moran discovered that she was the victim of a robbery. The two incidents portended tragedy. They also had the effect of dashing Ted Corkery's effort to defuse the itinerant issue.

Joe Murphy drowsily switched on the bedside lamp and glanced at his wristwatch at a quarter to seven, three-quarters of an hour before his usual rising-time. He was conscious of having been suddenly awakened, but he didn't know by what. There was a bleat, loud, intrusive. 'In heaven's name, what was that?' asked Sandra. Joe stepped out of bed, went to the window, opened the curtains, and looked into two horizontal black slits, the unblinking eyes of a goat. In the background he could see two large shapes.

'Good Christ!' he exclaimed, quickly turning away from the window.

'What is it?' Sandra asked. Joe didn't reply. Pulling on a dressing-gown he rushed from the bedroom.

He drove the goat and two horses from the garden. When daylight came he inspected the damage: hoof-chopped lawn, scratched wall coping, trampled flower beds, chewed shrubs. He could have sworn he had closed the gate the previous night. His nearest neighbours had had a similar experience.

Joe bolted his breakfast. He had decided against telephoning the gardai. He would call to the garda station personally and insist on seeing the superintendent. He had put up with enough: the assault on Jacqueline, the blonde bitch practically accusing him of rape, and now the destruction of his property by marauding goats and horses. The way things were going, they might as well all pull out and let the tinkers take over the place.

———————

Helen Moran sensed that something was amiss in the living room. She had just returned home after attending Mass and completing her shopping. Her walk to and from town had been enjoyable: the day was sunny and bracing, a breath of spring in winter.

She scanned the room. Scattered near the fireplace were sprigs of holly, berries pinpricking the light brown carpet. She raised her eyes to the mantlepiece. Panic stabbed her. The vases were gone, the pair of enamelled spill vases. Family heirlooms, bone china.

Maybe I meant to clean them. I'm always forgetting things. Still in her overcoat, Helen rushed to the kitchen. The window over the sink was open. The back door was unlocked. An ormolu clock and silver were missing from the sitting room. The contents of drawers and wardrobe were strewn around her bedroom. Letters written by her husband, which she had preserved in a jewellery case, lay crumpled and torn on the bed. Nauseated, she lurched to the bathroom.

There, the intruder, or one of the intruders, had left a calling card—a stool afloat in the toilet bowl.

———————

After a heated interview with the superintendent, Joe drove to his office, where he phoned Councillor Lehane to ascertain the outcome of the Town Council's December meeting which had taken place the night before.

As he pondered his conversations with the two men, Joe had to restrain himself from sweeping the unopened post from his desk. He snapped at his employees. Seasonal jingles from a nearby shop grated on his nerves.

Because of the absence of a pound in Fernboro, the superintendent had said, the gardai could do little about wandering animals. It was no use prosecuting the tinkers because it probably would be impossible to prove who actually owned the animals. In any case, it was difficult to collect fines from tinkers. The superintendent had promised to do his best. He would send a couple of his men out to the camp.

His best is not fecking well good enough, fumed Joe. Who's going to pay for the damage to my garden?

Councillor Lehane had said the Town Council meeting was a wash-out. The Council was still awaiting a report on the tinker problem from the Town Clerk, Jack Power. Power's excuse for the delay was that he was awaiting clarification of legal points. Lehane had promised to keep up the pressure but he doubted if any action would be taken against the tinkers before Christmas.

Before Christmas! For Christ's sake, that means the tinkers'll hang around till summer. The phone rang.

'Yes,' Joe spat into the receiver.

'Mrs Moran has been robbed,' Sandra said.

'I'll be there in a few minutes,' said Joe, replacing the receiver after hearing the details. He resolved to call an emergency meeting of the Residents' Association for that night. Gardai or no gardai, Council or no Council, the tinkers would have to be taught a lesson.

By the time he had sat into his Audi, Joe's anger had cooled. He was out of the bunker, on the fairway, shooting straight for the green, and, by God, he wasn't going to be beaten.

———

'They didn't even flush the toilet. They hadn't the manners to do that. They didn't flush the toilet!'

When Joe reached home that morning, he had found Helen Moran inside. Sandra and Garda Breen were trying to console her. Deathly pale, eyes vacant, Helen mystified them with repetitive, obsessive references to a toilet. Sandra called a doctor. The doctor and Detective Prendergast arrived together. Joe asked the detective when he was going to make an arrest.

'We have first to find those responsible,' replied the detective.

'But isn't it obvious?' exclaimed Joe. 'The camp is just behind Mrs

Moran's house.'

Detective Prendergast gratefully accepted a cup of tea from Sandra and lowered his heavy body on to a chair. He had long ago become resigned to the fact that the world was full of would-be detectives.

The sight of the detective tranquilly drinking tea sorely tried Joe's patience. But he managed to control his voice. 'I mean, can there be any doubt about it? Antiques were taken. That crowd always goes for antiques. And Mrs Moran is out of the house around the same time every day. That crowd would know that.'

'We are taking all those factors into consideration,' said Detective Prendergast wearily. 'I have men searching the camp and I'm returning there now.'

'I'll come with you.'

'No, I don't think that would be advisable,' said Detective Prendergast, hastening to the hall door.

———————

In the seventeen days since his conversation with the Town Engineer, Ted Corkery had played on the image-conscious susceptibilities of his neighbours in River View Drive, and, where he judged it appropriate, he had selectively quoted, or occasionally misquoted, Fr Kearney's sermon. The message that Ted tried subtly to convey, with some success, was that respectable people, pillars of society, should be restrained and be seen to be restrained in their public behaviour, and should not be stampeded by others, who perhaps knew no better, into conduct that they would later regret. At this stage, casually, it seemed, he would glance towards Tuohy Place.

Ted's employees included men from Tuohy Place, some of whom, from long practice, were skilled builders, but they lacked certificates to prove the fact, and he paid them all as labourers. He was rabidly opposed to trade unions, although he'd once been a member of one himself. While expressing agreement with the men's animosity towards itinerants, he went on to suggest, in an apparently offhand manner, that they and the other tenants of Tuohy Place would be foolish to stick out their necks for people who a few years ago had demanded the construction of the Berlin Wall. He managed to imply that he had opposed the wall.

Now, as he waited amidst an overflowing crowd in Joe Murphy's sitting room for the emergency meeting of the Residents' Association to begin, Ted mentally admitted the failure of his Machiavellian tactics.

The crowd was in an ugly mood, incensed by rumours that throughout the day had gathered momentum and grown lurid in exaggeration. It was authoritatively and thrillingly asserted that not alone had Helen Moran been robbed, but that she had been viciously beaten by tinkers who had left her in a pool of blood. And not only that (voices lowered), she had been 'interfered with!' As for the horses, they had kicked Joe Murphy's little girl. In the face, somebody said. Disfigured for life, said another.

Joe Murphy, followed by Councillor Liam Lehane and Bill Sullivan, threaded his way through the crowd and, flanked by his two companions, took his Chairman's place behind the coffee table. The expressions of the three men were funereal. An expectant hush fell on the crowd. In the front row, notebook on knee, pen poised, sat Mossy Kenneally, the reporter. Joe tapped his Parker ball-point on the table, signalling the start of the meeting.

The signal wasn't heard by Helen Moran, because she was down the hallway, in the guest bedroom, sedated. Her daughter had promised to travel down from Dublin the next day.

———————

'I regret to say that no one has yet been arrested for the cowardly robbery, and…'

'We can't look crooked without being summonsed. But the knackers can get away with murder,' Jim Walsh shouted from the back of the room.

'Gardai how are ye! The gardai couldn't find honey in a beehive,' shouted someone else.

'Furthermore,' Joe continued, 'it appears to me that the authorities can do practically nothing about the problem of wandering animals. Undesirable elements are protected by the law while the rest of us have to fend for ourselves. And what is the Town Council doing? As far as I can see, sweet damn all!'

The meeting of the Residents' Association exploded into cries of Hear! Hear! and glares were directed at Councillor Lehane, who uncrossed his long legs. His Adam's apple jerked up and down. But he had to delay his performance.

Joe, fired by the shouts and cries, tipsy on the smoky, charged air, was trumpeting, 'My friends, are we going to stand by while elderly and frail members of our community are terrorised?'

'No-o!'

'Are we going to wait until someone—probably one of our children —is killed or maimed by their nags?'

'No-o!'

Noel Fitzharris, seated in the centre of the clamouring room, experienced a moment's claustrophobic panic as people all round him rose or half rose from their chairs. He removed his misted spectacles and wiped them on his handkerchief. Words of moderation in this atmosphere would be wasted, like shouting into a gale, he reflected sadly. But, he consoled himself, perhaps the meeting was serving a useful purpose, affording the residents a relatively harmless way of letting off steam. Besides, Murphy's demagoguery was rather comical. People resumed their seats and Noel put his spectacles back on. He saw with relief that Murphy had sat down.

It was Councillor Lehane's turn. He contrasted his own commitment with what he termed the 'timidity' of his fellow-Councillors on the itinerant problem; he avoided any direct criticism of the police but promised to acquaint the Minister for Justice with the 'harrowing' ordeals of law-abiding citizens in Fernboro; and he vowed to give unqualified support to any action that might be taken by the Residents' Association.

Jim Walsh led the cheers at the conclusion of Councillor Lehane's speech.

When the meeting ended two hours later, two proposals had been adopted.

Chapter 15

Mary McCarthy's thoughts swirled like the leaves at her feet as she walked down River Road. Anorak zipped against a south-westerly wind that zinged in the overhead electric wires, she had no destination in mind: she just wanted to get away from the camp for a while. Ahead she could see the lights of Fernboro. The atmosphere in the camp was tense: alcohol was intensifying the resentment caused by the events of the day. Mary was trying, with little success, to put these events into perspective.

Heinrich Obermeyer walked towards home, buffets of wind quickening his pace. He'd been to the factory, where production was at full stretch on an urgent export order. After dinner Carmel had dropped him off at work. She needed the car for a social call.

Figures converging in the night, Heinrich and Mary were a few yards apart when they recognised each other by the light of a street lamp. She immediately had an image of their previous meeting at the camp, over a month before, when Heinrich had shaken her hand. In her memory, Heinrich and that handshake were inextricable.

'Hello, sir,' she said, halting on the narrow footpath.

'Hello…Mary?'

'That's right, sir.' Her spirits rose. He remembered her name. 'A bad night.'

'Yes, it is a night to get in out of the weather. Well, I am glad to have seen you again.' Heinrich turned towards the avenue of his home.

A picture of the camp flashed into Mary's mind: of a draughty tent, of scowling, bickering men and women swaying and sprawling round a fire. She said impulsively, 'Sir, would you have a bit of sugar to spare?'

'It is not something that I carry in my pockets,' Heinrich said with a laugh. He thought for a moment, then added, 'But come on up to the house.'

Up the avenue they went, side by side, heads bent in contest with the wind that drowned the sound of their footsteps, Mary breaking into a trot now and then to compensate for Heinrich's longer strides. Once she almost slipped on wet leaves. He placed a steadying hand on her elbow and slowed his pace, rising still further in her estimation.

She wondered how Eamonn would react if he met her now. Supposing he was at home? He'd probably be frightened to see her with his father, afraid she'd say something about what happened after the dance. 'Twould serve him right. She couldn't swear that he was involved but he had fallen in her opinion like a statue tumbling from a pedestal.

'Here we are,' said Heinrich. He opened the door and switched on the hall light. Mary hovered on the threshold. That was as far as she had ever been.

'Are you not coming in?'

Mary stepped on to the springy carpet. Heinrich closed the door, reducing the wind to a murmur. He removed his overcoat and scarf and hung them on the hallstand. 'Through here,' he said, indicating a door at the end of the hallway. They entered the kitchen.

Mary paused again, an acolyte unsure of the next part of the ceremony. She could count on her fingers the number of times she had been inside a house. Opposite her was a Venetian-blinded window, and to its right, high on the soft-green-glossed wall, was a large picture of the Sacred Heart, under which glowed a cigar-shaped red light. The picture reassured her: it was something she could identify with, unlike the dials and switches of the electric cooker and dishwasher. The pine-panelled presses, the gleaming white fridge, the speckless chocolate-brown floor tiles, the solid-oak table with matching chairs, the glittering silver sink and taps, the twinkling delph in the grained-wood dresser—all these she scanned, and she heard the tock of the Roman-numeral pendulum clock and the singing of the kettle on the black-leaded range. Carmel and Heinrich had retained the range because they believed it was in character with the house and they enjoyed its homely aspect.

'Please, sit down,' said Heinrich. He opened a drawer in one of the presses and took out a tablecloth. Mary reached for the chair closest to her.

'No, not there. You will be more comfortable near the fire.' Mary obeyed.

Heinrich unfolded the cloth and spread it on the table. From the dresser he took cups and saucers and plates. He had loosened his tie and undone the top button of his shirt, over which he wore a vee-neck navy pullover; the jacket of his suit was draped on the back of a chair. Trying to appear casual, to put his guest at ease, he was racking his brains for a conversational gambit that would encourage her to talk freely. On the avenue he had suddenly conceived the idea of inviting her to the house: she could tell him about itinerants. From the inside.

When Heinrich had first seen itinerants, within a week of his arrival in Ireland, they had for him the attraction of a novelty. All of their caravans were horse-drawn then and he had supposed they were gypsies. Gypsies had become scarce on the continent: many had gone up the chimney.

Prior to his handshake with Mary, his sole connection with itinerants had been on a business level: he sold them scrap metal from the factory and they drove a hard bargain. He respected them for that. But the petition had illustrated his ignorance of these people: he didn't know enough to counter Murphy's arguments convincingly; he was unable even to influence Carmel. He had been ignorant in the past. Perhaps he hoped partially to expiate that sin of ignorance by talking to Mary, by learning from her the truth about itinerants.

There was another factor. Seeing Mary at the camp five or six weeks ago, seeing her under the street-lamp tonight, and now seeing her sitting at the kitchen table, Heinrich was drawn towards her in a way that puzzled him. It wasn't a sensual pull, though he experienced the usual nostalgic pang of middle-age at the sight of young comeliness. It was, he felt, something more.

He put cups and saucers and plates on the table. Then he extracted knives and spoons from a drawer.

'You're not making tea for me, sir!' A maid in the same house in the age of servants wouldn't have been more startled had her master assumed kitchen duties. Mary was not servile, but to her it just didn't seem right to witness Heinrich in such a domestic role: moreover, she couldn't remember ever having had a meal prepared for her by a man, certainly not by a male member of the quality.

'I am having some myself so you might as well join me. You are not in any hurry, are you?'

'No, sir, but...'

'Make yourself at home. We have the house to ourselves. There was no sound of a radio as we came in and that means that Eamonn, my son, is out. And my wife will not be back for a while. Anyway, she would be glad to see you here.'

Mary wasn't so sure about that. Nevertheless, her tension lessened and she surveyed with anticipation the plain and currant scones, the strawberry jam, and the assortment of biscuits that Heinrich laid on the table.

'I can make you a sandwich,' he offered. Mary declined. He poured the tea and sat down at right-angles to Mary, who had her back to the range. Trying to appear hungry, he buttered a scone and spread it thickly with jam: his guest, as he had intended, followed his lead.

By the time she was on her second cup of tea and fourth scone, Mary, prompted by Heinrich's polite questions and obvious interest, was chatting about her family, concentrating on Lukey's wedding which was to take place two days hence, on Saturday. Her voice, pleasant save for insufficient inflection, mingled with the hum of the wind, the click of cups on saucers, the occasional jingle of spoons. Then Heinrich said, 'So you are enjoying yourself with all the preparations for the wedding?'

Again Mary pictured the camp: silver-buttoned uniforms, silver-badged caps, gruff voices. She wanted to tell this man about things, really tell him, as opposed to the itinerant technique of whining a litany of woes.

'There wasn't much to enjoy today,' she said, unconsciously discarding the 'sir'. Heinrich was surprised by Mary's sudden loss of vivacity, and he had the urge to wipe from the corner of her mouth a smear of jam that almost matched the colour of her jumper.

She spoke of the robbery in Helen Moran's house, but concealed her lack of sympathy for Mrs Moran, whom she regarded as 'that snotty bitch with the cat'. Heinrich listened attentively, though he had already heard about the robbery from Carmel. As she talked, Mary's fingers crumbled a biscuit. She said, 'Of course, we were blamed for it.'

'Why do you say "of course"?'

'We—the travellers—are always blamed for everything.'

'Why is that?'

Mary didn't reply immediately. The movement of her fingers quickened, completing the dismemberment of the biscuit. Then she said hesitantly, 'Maybe it's because we are different...I mean...it's easy to pick us out.'

Heinrich understood her perfectly.

She related how the gardai had searched the camp that morning while most of the men were in town collecting their dole. Some of the men, including Ned, were later questioned in the barracks.

'One of the gardai, a big fella—I think Keogh's his name—shouted at me and accused me of breaking into the house. I denied it and I thought he'd hit me but I wasn't afraid. Even if I knew something, I wouldn't tell him. I'd tell them notten!'

Flushed, sitting upright, hands gripping the table-edge, Mary brushed a strand of hair away from her eyes, her expression full of defiance, pride and disdain.

And he suddenly understood why he was drawn towards this girl.

———————

Defiance and pride and disdain were in Adela Ornstein's expression on that morning. The morning after *Kristallnacht*. 10 November 1938.

Late in the night Heinrich had woken to light shimmering on the curtains of his bedroom window. Boots clumped in the street, and he heard shouts and the growl of a truck engine. Someone screamed. He heard the splintering crash of glass, and cheers. He looked out the window and saw flames and sparks leaping and shooting over rooftops. His father came into the room and forbade him to leave the house. Probably hooligans, his father said.

At breakfast the radio announced that people throughout the Reich had during the night spontaneously demonstrated their repugnance at the murder of a German diplomat by a Jew in Paris three days earlier.

Glass crunched under Heinrich's feet.

It was crunching under feet all over Germany that morning. The spontaneous demonstrators shattered so much glass that the night of their activities was eventually entitled the Night of Crystal.

Heinrich's destination was the big drapery store in Leopold Street. From a distance he saw a crowd around the store—housewives, Hitler Youth, a policeman, SA men with swastika armbands, loungers—and over the noise of traffic he heard jeers and laughter. He walked faster, almost breaking into a run.

Adela, wine pinafore bedraggled, left sleeve missing from her jumper, blood dripping from her hands, staining the slivers of glass she was picking from the pavement and depositing in a bin. Her father, shirt torn, head roughly bandaged, sweeping larger pieces of glass into a pile. Her mother, white blouse streaked with red, eyes swollen, on stage in the shop window without panes, rummaging for glass in scattered, trampled garments. SA men strutting, bellowing. Mannequins, limbless, wigless, naked, grotesque in the window and on the footpath.

People later said that the Ornsteins were lucky: their lives had been spared. Only one Jew had died in the town on *Kristallnacht*. Quite a few were injured. Only one building was burned: the synagogue. Not nearly as bad as other parts of the country, people said.

Adela saw Heinrich. Their eyes met. He took a step forward, then stopped. He stayed where he was. With the crowd. He averted his gaze.

Within a few weeks Jews were barred from German schools, and before the month was out, they were excluded from places of public recreation. Thus, Heinrich hadn't the option of meeting Adela, or so he reasoned, and he suppressed the inclination to do so.

Kristallnacht provided the knockout blow to the Ornsteins' business. They, and all German Jews, were forced to defray the cost of the damage caused by the spontaneous demonstrators.

Adela, petite, dark-haired, brown-eyed. Her expression surfaced to Heinrich's consciousness.

It annoyed him when he heard people claiming that they would change nothing if they could live their lives again. Such people, he believed, were either liars or downright stupid. If only he could start all over again, with a clean sheet. He would write a different story. Or would he? Could he? He was unable to decide how much of one's life was autobiography, how much biography.

———————

The clock's tock was loud in the kitchen. Mary wondered why Heinrich was staring at her like that with the eyes of a blind man. She coughed.

'I used to know a girl very like you,' he said.

'Did you ever dance with her?'

'Yes, as a matter of fact, I did. We learned to dance together; we grew up together.'

'Where is she now?'

'I wish I knew for sure.'

Almost unwittingly, Mary heard herself talking about the youth club dance. As she was explaining how she and her companions were refused entry a second time, Heinrich interjected, 'So far as I know my son was at that dance. He must not have seen what was going on. He would not have approved.'

Mary hesitated, but her respect for Heinrich prevented her from enlightening him, from pointing out to him the cracks in the statue. Instead she described the incident that had occurred after the dance.

'I heard glass breaking. That's what must have woke me up. Then something hit off the tent and something came in. We found out afterwards that it was a stone and it was the luck of God none of us was hit. Ann started to scream. And they were shouting. From what they were saying I knew it was someone who was at the dance. We could hear them running away. They broke windows in a few caravans.'

'Did you pick up the glass?' Heinrich asked. Mary looked uncomprehendingly at him.

He emerged from the time-warp. 'You said you knew these people had been at the dance from what they were shouting. What did they say?'

'Well, they said they would dance with us now...and other things.'

Heinrich recalled Carmel's comment that Eamonn had taken his time coming home from the youth club that night. She always kept an ear open for Eamonn when he was out late.

Wind funnelled into the hallway as the front door was opened. Mary jumped up from her chair. Carmel entered the kitchen, and stopped short.

'I'm just going, mam,' said Mary, and turned to Heinrich. 'Thanks, sir, for the tea…and everything.'

She was on the avenue before she remembered the sugar. Never previously had she forfeited material gain, however modest, through forgetfulness, and for some reason that she couldn't quite fathom, she was pleased.

'We were having a chat,' said Heinrich.

'I see. Well, I'm off to bed,' Carmel replied brusquely.

Chapter 16

Friday, 8 December. Feast of the Immaculate Conception of the Blessed Virgin Mary, the Mother of God. A Roman Catholic holyday. An overture to Christmas.

Shoppers crowded Fernboro from early morning.

Helen Moran was admitted to hospital. For observation, the doctor said.

Itinerants nursed cuts and bruises and hangovers; as Mary McCarthy had anticipated, a row had erupted in the camp during the night.

Joe Murphy and Councillor Liam Lehane met the Town Clerk in an effort to expedite measures against the itinerants.

Philip Shaw received a letter from Mr Donoghue, his employer. The letter, typed on Donoghue Corporation notepaper, arrived by the first post and contained, for Philip, the joyful news that business commitments would detain Mr Donoghue in the United States over Christmas.

'I would expect to be in Ireland before the end of the shooting season,' the letter continued. 'You are, no doubt, taking all necessary steps to ensure the well-being of my game birds. Major, in this regard it is important to be vigilant against trespassers. I'm sure I don't have to remind you that undesirables such as itinerants have no respect for

Fern Park or any property. You have my full authority to issue prosecutions for trespass if the need should arise.'

Two or three years ago, at a time when Mr Donoghue was in residence, dogs belonging to itinerants had chased the Fern Park peacock around the lawn. 'Major,' he had said witheringly, 'I never again want to see trash on my estate.'

An hour after reading the letter, Philip was parking his aged Land Rover outside the rectory gates in Upper Bridge Street. Across the street, in front of the courthouse, Joe Murphy was parking his Audi.

The reference to itinerants in Mr Donoghue's letter had reminded Philip that the Obermeyers were still awaiting his opinion on the petition; well, at least, Eamonn was. The boy had mentioned it on a number of occasions. Heinrich seemed to want to forget the matter and had apologised for what he termed his boorish behaviour. Philip had been rather taken aback by Heinrich's attitude during that Sunday dinner, but hadn't been offended. The chap had obviously drunk too much too quickly.

Reverend Cyril Wilson, sturdy, pepper-haired, answered the rectory door. In the drawing room he plugged in a one-bar electric fire and invited his visitor to sit down. They began to discuss parish affairs. Then Reverend Wilson asked Philip how he intended to spend Christmas.

Philip eased his chair closer to the electric fire. He said he would be dining with the Obermeyers on Christmas Day. They had been considering going to Germany for the festivities, but had decided to postpone the trip until Easter or the summer. He added, seemingly as an afterthought, 'Mention of the Obermeyers has brought something to mind. You may have heard or read about the petition regarding the itinerants. The Obermeyers were asked to sign it.'

'Speaking personally, I would not be in favour of such petitions,' said Rev Wilson who was also huddled close to the electric fire, his knees a few inches from Philip's. 'Some of our people live in River View Drive, near the itinerant camp, and I said the same thing to them. Fr Kearney—perhaps you know him?—is doing everything he can to defuse the situation and, of course, he deserves support.'

'What kind of support?' asked Philip.

'Well, our ladies are doing what they can by distributing necessities to the itinerants. Otherwise we have to be…how shall I put it? It is better that we should keep a low profile. No purpose would be served by drawing animosity on ourselves.'

'Animosity? I should have thought those days were gone.'

From the street came the drone of traffic, consisting mostly of cars conveying people to eleven o'clock Mass in St Bridget's. Reverend Wilson removed his elbows from his knees and straightened; the ruddiness of his features was heightened by the glow of the electric fire.

'Not entirely,' he said. 'For instance, you—a Protestant and ex-officer of the British army—would be ill-advised to get yourself involved in anything controversial. One should be careful not to mistake sufferance for tolerance.'

In the Town Council offices behind the Courthouse, Joe Murphy and Councillor Lehane were stressing to the Town Clerk, Jack Power, the need for regulations to prohibit the parking of caravans in the River Road area. One of the proposals adopted at the emergency meeting of the Residents' Association called for the immediate implementation of such regulations.

Joe and Councillor Lehane had arrived in the offices half an hour earlier. Power's devoted middle-aged secretary, Miss Byrne, informed them that he was not available at the moment, but when they said they would wait, she grudgingly supplied them with uncomfortable chairs.

She soon lapsed into silence, a silence broken occasionally by the rattle of her ancient massive black typewriter, and from time to time she eyed Joe, in his sheepskin car-coat, and Councillor Lehane, in his sky-blue anorak, as if she expected them to pilfer the files that occupied shelves lining one wall.

Dapper in a trench-coat, brown leather gloves, trilby, green scarf, and carrying a rolled-up black umbrella, Power strolled into the office to begin his day's work. Officially his hours of duty were from nine to five with an hour's break for lunch, but he was flexible in his interpretation of time. Anyway, he reasoned, Miss Byrne was more than capable of holding the fort. After expressing the hope that his visitors hadn't been waiting too long, he nonchalantly informed them that he'd been at ten o'clock Mass. He divested himself of gloves, coat, hat, and scarf, and handed them to Miss Byrne. Carefully patting strands of grey hair across his bald crown which was egg-white against the faded-parchment complexion of his face, Power sat into the swivel chair behind his desk, like a judge ready to hear a case.

'What can I do for you, gentlemen?' he asked in a tone of polite enquiry, the picture of patience, even though he had already made his mind up on the matter. Though it was a nuisance, one had to go through the motions of democracy.

'Well, Mr Power, let me explain why we are here,' began Councillor Lehane.

'I'm sure Mr Power is fully aware of why we are here,' Joe interjected. 'Let's have no more pussyfooting.'

Power, impassive but observant, was amused at Lehane's annoyance. Conscious of formalities, Councillor Lehane believed that as an elected representative of the people he was entitled to precedence over Joe, at least in the Town Council offices.

Joe, unaware of having committed a peccadillo, or more likely, not caring, was continuing. 'The Council is not living up to its responsibilities. It's the same story for all the authorities in this country. Someone will have to be seriously injured or worse before anything is done. This morning a lady was removed to hospital, an inoffensive lady terrorised out of her home. And there were people who didn't get a wink of sleep last night with the racket that was going on in the camp.'

'I assure you, Mr Murphy, that I have every sympathy with you in your unfortunate predicament,' Power said soothingly.

'You could have fooled me,' Joe snapped. 'We have been waiting over a month for you to prepare a report on the itinerants.'

'We encountered unforseen legal difficulties.'

'You don't have any legal difficulties in sending out your rate bills. Anyway, it's too late for reports. I'm too gentlemanly to suggest what you can do with your report.'

'And I'm too gentlemanly to take offence or to accede to your implied suggestion.' Power smiled briefly.

Joe Murphy was, for once, lost for words.

After almost thirty years as Town Clerk, Power regarded the Town Council as his fiefdom, to be ruled with the assistance of TJ Fennell and Miss Byrne. It was TJ who, without explaining why, had asked him to delay his report on the itinerant situation, and he had been glad to oblige, using legal difficulties as a smokescreen. Power was negative by nature, adept at interpreting rules to obstruct rather than to promote progress. As a result, the Council had a healthy bank balance while Fernboro suffered from patchy roads and footpaths, inadequate public lighting and decaying local authority houses.

Councillor Lehane, capitalising on Joe's temporary silence, was demanding the removal of caravans from River Road.

Demanding, no less! Power wanted to laugh out loud. He said, 'Regulations for the purpose of prohibiting the parking of caravans are fraught with legal implications.'

Joe regained control of his voice. 'Surely such regulations are not beyond the realms of possibility?'

'Other towns have them,' said Councillor Lehane.

'Circumstances vary from place to place,' Power said. 'Besides, the regulations cannot even be drafted without first obtaining the formal approval of the Council.'

'Which means waiting for another month,' Joe retorted, 'and God knows how long we'd have to wait after that for the regulations actually to come into force.'

'Regretfully, that is an accurate summary of the situation,' Power declared.

Joe leaped to his feet, overturning his chair. He rushed out the door, not halting until he reached his car. Councillor Lehane followed, after diplomatically wishing Power good morning.

Chapter 17

On Saturday they were off to Lukey McCarthy's wedding. The small minority relying on horse-drawn transport had departed during the previous few days. Lukey was to marry Thrush Stokes in a town almost twenty miles away.

Vans left the camp, washed specially for the occasion, bumpers and hub-caps gleaming, some beribboned, all low on axles with the weight of men and women and children in their best clothes. Down River Road they sped, horns blaring. To Tom and Maggie McCarthy—he in a red tie, yellow shirt and brown suit, she in wine costume, frilled cream blouse with Tara brooch at the neck—the din was a triumphant fanfare. Their son was marrying, and not only that, he was marrying a Stokes, and it wasn't everyone who was good enough for the Stokeses.

The occupants of the vans didn't know when they would return to the camp. Time, never of pressing concern to them, was inconsequential when there were bottles and barrels to be emptied, food to be eaten, dances to be danced, songs to be sung, stories to be told. The Stokeses knew how things should be done and they had hired a hall for the wedding reception.

By early afternoon all the vans had vacated the camp.

Two hours later, Joe Murphy, accompanied by Bill Sullivan, Councillor Lehane, and Jim Walsh, cruised by the camp in his Audi.

Donkeys and dogs and horses and wisps of smoke from caravan stove-pipes were, so far as they could see, the only signs of life.

'Are you sure they're all gone?' Joe asked.

'Of course I'm sure. Didn't I tell you they were all gone to the wedding?' said Jim, self-important.

'I suppose we'll never get a better chance than this,' Joe said.

Tempers, already short, were soured by the sight of the shining vans streaming along River Road. Vans driven by men who had robbed Helen Moran. She was seriously ill in hospital, people said. Dangerously ill, some said. Dying, others said. And the gardai hadn't arrested anyone.

Aware of the exodus from the camp and still smarting from his abortive encounter with the Town Clerk on the previous day, Joe Murphy called a meeting of the officers of the Residents' Association. The second proposal adopted at the Association's emergency meeting on Thursday night empowered the officers to take whatever steps they deemed necessary in furtherance of the anti-itinerant campaign.

The officers approved Joe's suggestion that he should lead what he called a 'reconnaissance mission' to the camp. Councillor Lehane, alerted by Jim Walsh, arrived just as the mission was setting out, and he joined it. Sitting in the Audi's front passenger seat, Councillor Lehane was congratulating himself on being in the right place at the right time.

While Councillor Lehane was stretching like a contented cat in the Audi, his arch-rival, Councillor Oliver Dooley, was being admitted to the home of Hugh McDonald, Fernboro's TD. Councillor Dooley was shown into a room off the hall.

'I am glad you could come,' said McDonald. 'Please, sit down. Make yourself comfortable. What will you have to drink? Brandy?'

At a side table he poured a large measure for his visitor, and for himself, a small one which he liberally diluted with ginger ale. He was low-sized, square-faced with mild blue eyes, and he had a shock of white hair that matched his moustache. He was impeccably attired in a dark grey three-piece suit, blue shirt, and navy tie. Someone recently remarked that he bore a resemblance to Lloyd George, a comparison that he publicly deprecated. Privately it pleased him.

'Won't you take off your coat?' he asked, handing Councillor Dooley a bulbous glass. The latter, who was sitting in an armchair near the fireplace where turf and logs blazed, unbuttoned his Crombie but didn't remove it. He didn't know how long he would be staying. Indeed he had no idea why McDonald had asked him to call. Though members of the same political party, they were not friends.

While his host was pouring drinks, Councillor Dooley scanned with a touch of envy framed photographs hanging over the mantelpiece and on the walls. The photographs traced McDonald's career from the time he was first elected to the Dáil forty years before, showing in acceleration the transformation of a rookie into a venerable party elder, and including a picture of him as a minister complete with rolled-up umbrella and hard hat.

'Ah, you've been looking at my photographs, an old man's vanity,' said McDonald, sitting into an armchair opposite Councillor Dooley. 'I'm afraid the set is complete.'

Hope kindled in Councillor Dooley. 'Oh, surely not!' he said.

'I wanted you to be among the first to know, and I wanted you to hear it from myself. I will not be going for re-election.' McDonald didn't reveal, nor did he intend to, that his retirement from the Dáil was being forced. Party leaders were shedding the old men.

'This is…is shocking news. Won't you reconsider?' Colour was rising in Councillor Dooley's already sanguine visage, and he gulped his brandy.

A cynical smile creased McDonald's face for a split second. 'There is no possibility of my reconsidering,' he said. 'I have decided to let someone else have a chance, though it goes without saying that I am willing to place my experience and advice at the disposal of my replacement, whoever he or she may be. Thanks all the same for your expression of concern. Let me give you a refill.'

Having replenished his guest's glass, McDonald resumed his seat.

'I think I'll take off my coat,' said Councillor Dooley. He hung the coat on the back of the chair which he moved back from the heat of the fire. Hitching up the legs of his pinstripe trousers, he settled into the chair. He took a sip of brandy and said, 'Your replacement—whoever that may be—is sure to be elected. It's a safe party seat.'

'Yes. The important thing is to win the party nomination.'

'Of course, you would have a big say in that. You control the party organisation, or most of it, around here.'

'I wouldn't go so far as to say that, but I suppose I have a certain amount of influence.' McDonald picked up a poker and prodded at the fire.

'There is bound to be a lot of competition for the nomination. Liam Lehane, for instance,' said Councillor Dooley.

McDonald nodded non-committally. Recalling his own modest origins and success against the odds, he was sympathetically, even affectionately, disposed towards Lehane, and he had intended to try and secure the nomination for him. Besides, he was sure that a grateful Lehane would prove to be a pliable successor. But Lehane's Hitler remark about the itinerants had been picked up by the national newspapers and by radio and television, and had severely embarrassed party headquarters. McDonald disliked headquarters, which, he believed, was infiltrated by ungodly liberals, but he realised that it was unlikely to sanction Lehane as a party Dáil candidate.

Councillor Dooley finished his brandy, and toying with the glass, said quickly and quietly, 'I wouldn't mind having a shot at it myself.' He added, 'But it's no use going forward without a reasonable chance of success. I have my legal business to consider.'

'Yes, very true…very true.'

'I would appreciate your advice.'

'Your glass is empty.'

Councillor Dooley put a hand over the glass. 'No, no, I have enough for the moment,' he said.

McDonald, who had half-risen, sat back. 'I have been following your political progress with interest,' he said, 'particularly your contributions to Council meetings. I notice, for instance, that you have a lot to say about Fern Heights. You don't seem to approve of what is happening up there?'

Councillor Dooley was puzzled but he sensed the importance of not answering wrongly. But what would constitute a wrong answer? He equivocated. 'It's not so much that I don't approve; really, I don't know what is happening there.'

McDonald did know what was happening: he was one of the

investors (secret) in the Fern Heights development, and Ted Corkery, the contractor, had asked him to stop Dooley 'poking his nose' into the scheme.

'I believe that quite a number of houses will be built at Fern Heights,' said McDonald. 'The sale of the houses will involve a substantial amount of legal work. But unnecessary publicity could delay the whole scheme. I am thinking of the people who are anxious to purchase the houses. I don't have to tell you that they wouldn't appreciate such a delay. We, as public representatives, should do everything in our power to facilitate people who are willing to purchase homes of their own. Don't you agree?'

'Yes, wholeheartedly.'

'Good, I believe we understand each other. Now, I insist that you have another drink.'

Councillor Dooley felt like a weak swimmer who, after being out of his depth, finds packed sand under his feet. He wasn't sure how he had reached shore, but he was safe. 'I wonder could I have a chaser?' he asked. McDonald filled him a glass of lager.

The lager spread a delicious coolness through Councillor Dooley.

Reconnaissance mission completed, Joe Murphy re-convened the officers of the Residents' Association. They met in his home. Eight or nine non-officer members of the Association, breathing an air of expectancy, anxious to miss nothing, were there too. Darkness was falling and Joe had switched on the light, but hadn't drawn the curtains. Passers-by could see him, gesticulating, flushed and serious, and though they couldn't hear what he was saying, they surmised its importance.

'Everyone here should contact his or her neighbour,' Joe was saying. 'It's essential that we have as many people there as possible.'

'I couldn't agree with you more,' said Councillor Lehane. 'The more people you have the better. It's vitally necessary to demonstrate the depth of public feeling on this issue, and needless to say, I'm with you all the way.'

'Is everyone in agreement?' Joe asked. Heads nodded and voices assented. He continued, 'Right, we will assemble outside Mrs Moran's house at half-seven. Is that time suitable? Good. And bring flashlamps with you. I think that's everything arranged. Oh, I was nearly forgetting. We'll need a tractor. Leave that to me. I know where we can get one.'

Chapter 18

The calendar girl in the minuscule bikini had donned a cuddly, though skimpy, Santa Claus cloak: that was the only indication that a month had passed since Heinrich's last visit to his son's room. As before, Heinrich was on a chair, facing Eamonn, who was seated on the side of the bed.

The only sound in the room was Heinrich's voice, low but clear. Keeping his gaze on Eamonn's face, he spoke about the stone-throwing incident at the itinerant camp after the dance, omitting mention of his conversation with Mary McCarthy two nights previously.

Despite reasoning that there was probably a perfectly logical explanation for Eamonn's late homecoming from the dance—he had been with a girl, most likely—Heinrich couldn't rid himself of a nagging suspicion. He hadn't confided his suspicion in Carmel who, in any case, had been irritated when he tried to raise the subject of Mary McCarthy. His son's cleverness at school—he was especially gifted at languages—didn't dazzle Heinrich into complacency. He recalled his own father who had also been linguistically gifted.

The bed creaked as Eamonn shifted position. He had been directly underneath the light, strands of his hair burnished to russet. 'Where did you hear about this?' he asked.

'That is not important. Why did you throw stones at the camp?'

'What makes you think I was involved?'

'Your demeanour is enough. You cannot look me straight in the eye.'

Boys and girls, prolonging the exhilaration of the dance, chirruped around tables in Dino's. Two waitresses, in short skirts and white plastic aprons, looking like children long past their bedtime, but conscious of boys' eyes on their thighs, ferried plates from the counter behind which Dino and his wife laboured.

Several girls wasted smiles on Eamonn. He answered their greetings monosyllabically. Senan Murphy and Cathal Corkery, while sociable, didn't offer to escort any of the girls home. They complained that the 'good things'—girls generous with their favours—were all booked. The three friends lingered over cups of coffee until Dino began switching off lights.

'I've got an idea,' said Senan, when they reached the street. 'Come on. I'll explain it as we go along.' Their footsteps echoed hollowly in the late-night stillness. 'You heard what that knacker bitch said to my father tonight. You'd think he had raped her. As if anyone in their right sense would touch her with a long pole.'

It was only now that Senan's anger at the incident became apparent. He had raised the subject earlier, just after the dance, but without dwelling on it.

'Ah, nobody took any notice of what she said,' Cathal consoled him.

'That's easy to say, but how would you feel if those things were said about your old man?' Senan retorted. He outlined his idea. Cathal responded enthusiastically. At Gradys pub they turned right, into River Road.

'Maybe we should just go home,' Eamonn said.

'Are you afraid?' asked Senan, who, like his father, was stockily built. He stopped and scrutinised Eamonn.

'Our Eamonn's in love,' laughed Cathal. 'Did you not see the way he and that little sexy black-haired bit were looking at each other in the hall?'

'In love with a knacker! A knacker-lover!' Senan rolled the words on his tongue. Then he and Cathal, hooting, pranced around Eamonn.

'There's no need to talk shit,' said Eamonn, pretending to laugh. 'I'm ready. Let's go.' He began to walk rapidly.

Treading lightly on their soles, they passed the line of caravans. In the air was a whiff of woodsmoke, although no fire was in sight. Eamonn's toe scuffed a tin can and it clattered long and loud. Dogs barked. Alongside the road was something black and large and snorting. A horse.

When they rounded the bend beyond the camp, they halted and breathed deeply. Eamonn wished that he were somewhere else, preferably in bed, and he suspected that the others did too. Senan lit a cigarette and the flare of the match momentarily darkened the night. 'We'll get ammunition here,' he said, stooping and gathering stones from the gravelly margin of the road.

Keeping close to one another, they started back towards the camp. 'Now!' hissed Senan.

Eamonn raised his right arm, aiming in the general direction of the caravans. He visualised Mary, supine, her fingers touching the stone, curling round it. 'I'll dance with you now.' His own words surprised him. Dogs snarled, fighting to get free of the ropes to which they were tied. Glass shattered.

'You stinking knackers.' 'Dirty whores,' Senan and Cathal were shouting. A light went on in a caravan.

Eamonn sobbed with the effort of running so fast away from the camp, and in his mind he could see itinerants, brawny, brutal men. His sobs mingled with those of Senan and Cathal, counterpointing the pound of their feet. The distance seemed to be interminable, but at last they reached the avenue to Eamonn's home and flung themselves in among the trees, into the deeper darkness.

An engine started and as its sound grew louder the three friends crouched lower. A van cruised by, heading towards the town, headlamps probing the branches of trees. It returned shortly afterwards and they caught a glimpse of its tail-lights. From the camp came the sound of voices.

The night grew quiet, save for their intermittent whispers, and they shivered in the chilly air. As Eamonn parted from Senan and Cathal he was glad of the darkness that hid their faces.

His behaviour at the camp had given Eamonn a new insight into his own character. He shied from it. He tried to dismiss his conduct as an aberration, and sought consolation in the recollection that he, unlike his friends, hadn't used abusive language towards the itinerants.

As for Mary McCarthy, he told himself that she wasn't so attractive when you saw her up close: she was too small, she smudged her lipstick, her accent was rough. An infatuation, that's what it had been. Really, he didn't care for her at all. Then he remembered how he had felt as he had thrown the stone and he ached for her, was ashamed of the pain.

———————

'It was only a prank,' said Eamonn. Immediately conscious of the ineptitude of the remark, he wished that he could withdraw it, but couldn't think of anything better to say.

The silence in the bedroom became oppressive and he ventured a glance at Heinrich, hoping to elicit some response.

'A prank?' parroted Heinrich, as if he had been given a cue he didn't understand.

'I mean...we meant no harm.'

Heinrich was struck by a feeling of despair, a terrible fear that his son was no better than he himself was. He straightened in his chair and groped for a spark of reassurance. 'Did you intend to break the windows, the windows in the caravan?'

'No. I didn't, anyhow.'

'Well, at least, that is something to be thankful for, that and the fact that nobody was injured.'

'There was no question of anyone being hurt.'

'A girl from the camp told me differently. She said a child was almost hit by a stone.'

'What girl?' asked Eamonn, meeting his father's eyes.

'Mary McCarthy. She was here on Thursday night.' Heinrich noticed a barely perceptible flicker of his son's eyes, a faint blush. Eamonn shifted again, further away from the light, but he was grateful to his father for saying that name, for pronouncing it without a leer.

'Luckily for you and your friends neither she nor anybody else in the camp saw who threw the stones,' said Heinrich. Then, in a quick aside, 'She is a very pretty girl.'

'Mary McCarthy? Yes, I suppose she is.'

'So you know her?'

'Only to see her.' Eamonn's voice took on an edge. 'She's an itinerant.'

'Heinrich, because the Ornsteins are Jews, their situation—unfortunate though it is—has to be regarded in the context of certain historical, philosophical, and, if I may say so, theological processes, quite apart altogether from political considerations.'

His father's words were uttered with an obvious effort at sincerity, but to Heinrich they sounded condescendingly apologetic, and were meaningless, offering him none of the sustenance, none of the assuagement, none of the wisdom that he craved. His father's study was full of the fruits of centuries of human wisdom. Darkness was falling and logs flamed and crepitated on the hearth. Gilt-tooled spines reflected the flames, Aristotle, Plato, Aquinas, Shakespeare, Schiller, Goethe. Volumes from floor to ceiling, a book-walled room. Heinrich's father was seated at an escritoire, the right side of his lean, sallow face mottled in the firelight, the left side in shadow. In this study, where books soaked and softened the noise of the outside world, he dealt with the foreign correspondence of Obermeyer Industries, while, as a major shareholder in the firm, his wealth rose with the tide of Nazi rearmament.

Heinrich was seated on the other side of the escritoire, his mind still seared by the glance that Adela had cast at him that morning as she gathered glass from the pavement.

He had abandoned her there, in Leopold Street, to laughter and jeers, to sheepish stares. He walked through streets, along country roads, through stubble fields, telling himself that he could have done nothing to help her and her parents. Other than drawing attention to himself, no purpose would have been served by his intervention. What could he have done? Talked with the Ornsteins? What could he have said? Assisted them in picking up glass? The SA and police would probably have stopped him. Wiped blood from Adela's hands? Would she have allowed him to do so? Why hadn't the police protected the Ornsteins?

Heinrich hadn't swallowed the sophism, incorporated in official teaching, that the state, because it was the state, was always right, but neither had he enquired into it closely, involving, as it did, questions about the nature of the Third Reich.

No, no…none of this would have happened if that Jew hadn't killed our diplomat in Paris.

Then Adela's glance again filled his mind.

He hurried back to town, to Leopold Street, where, surprised by the normality of the scene, he joined the flow of pedestrians whose footfalls fused with the clip-clop of dray-pulling horses and the coughs of car- and truck-engines. Lights were coming on in shop windows.

No lights were coming on in Ornsteins' drapery store.

Heinrich halted at the store, on the glass-free footpath. *Juden*. The word was daubed in yellow paint on the boarded-up display window. He looked up at the first and second-floor windows. They were in darkness.

He had to talk to someone. He went home to his father.

The friendship of Heinrich and Adela—he was a year the senior —was, so to speak, inherited. It began when they toddled towards each other from their fathers' coat-tails. Their fathers, who had similar intellectual tastes, frequently exchanged visits and ideas and books. Within the previous two years or so, these exchanges had become less frequent, then ceased.

Contact between Heinrich and Adela had also decreased, which wasn't fully explained by the fact that she had stopped going to the cinema, concerts, and student dances. As young children they had been seemingly inseparable, two dark-haired youngsters, absorbed in their private world, often precociously holding hands, drawing benign smiles from the townspeople. The smiles had lost their benignity, had mostly disappeared altogether. And Heinrich withheld his hand, at least in public, where, although he would have denied it, he preferred not to be seen with Adela. She, of course, sensed this and began treating him with a coolness that was foreign to her usually extrovert nature. He, instead of trying to dispel this coolness, which he knew was justified, adopted a similar attitude towards her.

Entering the Ornstein store became an ordeal for Heinrich, as much of an ordeal as it had once been a pleasure. The store had been a magical place then, bustling with customers. Now it was an echo-chamber for passing traffic, a place where Herr and Frau Ornstein vainly tried to convey the impression of being busy. They would look at Heinrich, questioningly, he thought, bewilderment and hurt in their eyes. His visits to the store tailed off.

Heinrich longed to regain the warmth that had been part of his attachment to Adela, and so, he believed, did she. He was acutely aware that the first move was up to him, but he held back.

Heinrich's father picked up a book that had been lying open on the escritoire. He held the volume in his left hand, using his forefinger as a bookmark, and his right hand fondled the cover. He continued, 'As regards political considerations, I think we can have reason for optimism. As you may know, I am no apologist for the present regime, but one has to understand that it is still in the process of consolidating its position and this always entails some disruption. However, judging from historical precedent, I am confident that moderation will ensue from the responsibility of government. Therefore, we should not read too much into the incidents of last night, unsavoury though they were.'

Heinrich rose from his chair, stood for a few moments, then sat beside his son on the bed.

'Eamonn, on the last occasion I was in this room I said something to the effect that I did not need pictures to tell me what happened—do you remember?—and later, on the Sunday we went for a walk, you asked me what I had meant by that statement.'

A knock on the front door was barely audible in the bedroom, its resonance absorbed by the carpeted hallway and stairs.

'I shall try to explain that statement to you now.'

Carmel opened the front door, admitting Philip Shaw, who asked, 'I say, Carmel, have you any idea what is going on at the camp? I noticed a lot of activity up there as I was driving past.'

Chapter 19

'I never told you that I was in Russia. I was there for over a year,' said Heinrich.

'In Russia?' Eamonn said, as if he had difficulty in assimilating the information, but eager for the next instalment.

'I trust you to keep the fact between ourselves, not to mention it to Philip, for instance. It is not a period of my life suited to leisurely reminiscence.' Heinrich paused, then asked, 'In your reading did you ever come upon references to special units, *Sonderkommandos*?'

'No, I don't think so.'

'If you had, you would remember. Their activities are not easily forgotten. The commandos were components of larger groups, *Einsatzgruppen*, which were attached to the German army groups in Russia. That is not to say that all commandos were German. The unit that I…that I came across included Lithuanians and Ukrainians. The main purpose of the commandos was to fight partisans—or so we were told.'

Heinrich spoke dispassionately, as though he were a disinterested listener to his own words which, to his surprise, flowed forth calmly. And already he was experiencing a sense of release.

'A lot of people, thousands, were dealt with in commando actions and were disposed of in pits. The aim was to have everything done on a methodical basis. Later, though, when the war was turning against us, the pits were reopened and the bodies burned in an attempt to wipe out the evidence. Eamonn, are you beginning to see the picture?'

'Yes.' Eamonn's reply was barely audible.

'The *Sonderkommandos* executed men, women, and children, usually by shooting, though on rare occasions specially adapted vans were used to gas people, or rather, to suffocate them. The majority of the victims were Jews, but in some places the inmates of asylums and orphanages were also eliminated.'

'But why? Why did all this happen?'

'Why? When you think about it, I suppose that even prejudice has a logical conclusion. The commandos were instruments in bringing about that conclusion. Quite a number were ordinary policemen by profession and, of course, there were also office and technical staff. One *Einsatzgruppe* was actually commanded by an intellectual, Otto Ohlendorf.'

'These commando actions…did you ever see one?'

Heinrich stole a sideways glance at his son, who was pulling a fibre from the multi-hued candlewick bedspread, his jeans and jumper dark-blue in contrast with the sky-blue of his eyes—ingenuous eyes, inviting candour. That was Heinrich's impression, and the impulse to unburden himself was almost overwhelming. He replied, 'I couldn't very well avoid seeing them.'

'Why didn't you…why didn't the army intervene?'

'Oh, the army intervened all right. In many instances the army assisted the commandos,' retorted Heinrich who, perversely irritated at Eamonn for his lack of perceptiveness, wanted to grab him by the shoulders, shake him, shout at him: I was a *Sonderkommando*! Me, your father. A *Sonderkommando*! Instead, he added, 'As for me, I was a mere Lieutenant at the time. Field Marshals such as von Manstein and von Reichenau, who to us were God-like personages—but I do not have to tell you that; you are a connoisseur of German generals—issued orders to us in which they stressed the necessity for revenge on what they called sub-human Jewry.'

Eamonn looked around his room and then his gaze rested on his father. Outrage battled with morbid curiosity in his mind.

'"When the ends are great, humanity employs other standards and no longer judges crime as such even if it resorts to the most frightful means",' Heinrich said softly, as though he were speaking to himself. His irritation had faded as rapidly as it had arisen. 'I always remember that from Nietzsche.'

'Oh fu...' Eamonn checked himself just in time; his father disliked swearing. 'Nietzsche! I don't want to hear what he said or what the Generals said. What did *you* think as you saw people being murdered?'

'I tried not to think. Most of us tried not to think.'

'But you must have thought something.'

'I know that it is probably difficult for you to understand but one does that, one suppresses one's thoughts when the outcome of such thoughts is likely to be unpleasant. It is a way of maintaining sanity. There were men, comrades of mine, who believed, or claimed to believe, that it was all because of the war, that the people executed by the commandos were inevitable casualties of war.'

'Heinrich! Philip is here.' Carmel's voice penetrated Eamonn's room.

'Well, Eamonn, I hope you will not think too badly of me,' said Heinrich, rising to his feet. He was glad of an excuse to leave the room, yet unwilling to depart. He waited for a few moments, but Eamonn didn't reply.

As he reached the door, Heinrich said, 'I am sure I can rely on you not to throw any more stones.'

His father gone, Eamonn lay back on the bed, preparatory to sorting his thoughts. Then, seemingly of its own volition, his gaze wandered to and lingered on the calendar girl, the nicest Santa Claus he'd ever seen, a promise of things to come. Her image was for him an affirmation of life. Hungry for music, the music of his generation, he switched on the transistor.

Heinrich halted at the head of the stairs. There was no escape. The sense of release he had experienced while speaking with Eamonn had completely evaporated: a deliberately imperfect confession was without possibility of absolution. From below, up the shadowy, curved stairwell, came the murmur of voices, Philip's predominating; and

145

then, from behind, from Eamonn's room, came muffled music, the staccato of drums.

No escape from the *Sonderkommandos*. The thought dismayed Heinrich. The bond of the commandos condemned him to hypocrisy. The *Sonderkommandos* were thus closer to him than his son or his wife.

Down the stairs he hurried, away from the atavistic drumbeats. He glanced into the mirror on the hallstand, at his reassuringly unchanged countenance. In the living room he exchanged greetings with Philip, then went to the sideboard where he poured himself a generous brandy.

'Philip says something is going on at the camp,' said Carmel, who was in a fireside armchair. Philip, glass in hand, was seated opposite her. Heinrich moved forward a few paces and placed his left hand on the back of Carmel's chair. Philip took up the story.

When he'd finished, Carmel asked, 'Eamonn didn't come down with you? Is he still in his room?'

Heinrich nodded.

'Well, I think it's better to say nothing to him about this,' she said. 'We don't want him going near the camp.'

Philip nodded agreement but Heinrich said, 'Are you not being alarmist? Remember we heard the vans this morning? The activity is probably connected with the wedding.'

He topped up Philip's glass and poured himself a drink, but the brandy failed to dissolve a vague, persistent feeling of apprehension in his stomach. Moving to sit on the arm of Carmel's chair, he reminded himself that he was, after all, in Ireland, in Fernboro.

The knock on the front door was gentle. Carmel looked at Heinrich and Philip for confirmation that she had heard aright, then went into the hallway.

'You're very welcome.' Carmel's cordial tones drifted through the partially open door. Heinrich and Philip strained to make out the topic of conversation, to identify the caller.

'Thank you...telephone...would appreciate that.' The voice was male, soft. Heinrich didn't recognise it. He looked at Philip and shrugged.

Whirr of the telephone dial. Then Carmel. 'Hello. Garda Station? Hold on, please.' Heinrich took a gulp of brandy. He now wished that

Carmel had fully closed the door, yet suppressed the urge to do so himself.

'Yes...police intervention...advisable...trouble,' said the male voice. A bell tinkled, indicating that he had hung up the phone.

'Of course, you must come in and warm yourself.'

Carmel entered the room and held the door open for a man who, tortoise-like, peered out of a long, heavy, dark-brown overcoat. For a moment, it seemed that his head was about to retract at the sight of Heinrich and Philip.

'This is Mr Fitzharris,' said Carmel, her hand on his left elbow, steering him towards the fire.

Though she had for him that affection that one retains for the kind personalities of one's earliest years—he had lived only a few fields away from her childhood home and had been a friend of her parents —Carmel didn't even contemplate using his Christian name. To her he had always been 'Mr Fitzharris', and always would be. After he'd moved to River View Drive, following the sale of his farm to her brother Peter, she had on numerous occasions invited him to call. She had been disappointed by his failure to avail of the invitation, and it had crossed her mind that perhaps he hadn't called because he was angered by Peter's demolition of the Fitzharris homestead, an action that had enraged her. But on reflection she dismissed this surmise; Mr Fitzharris wasn't the type to apportion blame where it didn't belong. She had concluded that Mr Fitzharris was probably wholly contented with his own company and that of his books.

Noel Fitzharris shook hands with Heinrich and Philip, and, pressed by Carmel, consented to unbutton his coat and sit into an armchair. He accepted a whiskey from Heinrich and sipped it, hoping that its medicinal properties would help him to overcome a deep tiredness that afflicted limb and brain, the trough after an emotional high. The tiredness, a physical weakness, annoyed him because it prevented him from returning to the camp immediately. He had rushed here from the camp, reasoning that the nearest telephone was probably in the Obermeyer house, or, as he thought of it, Carmel Ahern's house. Despite Carmel's invitations, he hadn't visited the house previously because, not knowing her husband, he felt that he might be intruding.

'Mr Fitzharris is very worried about the situation at the camp,' said

147

Carmel, perched on the right arm-rest of Philip's chair.

'Yes, I got that impression. Philip and I could not help overhearing part of the telephone conversation,' said Heinrich, who was standing by the mantelpiece.

'What precisely is going on, Mr Fitzharris?' Philip asked.

He explained that he had come upon the scene at the camp as he was returning home from a walk. He described it and said he had attempted to intervene but was repulsed in no uncertain terms, in language best left to the imagination.

'Phoning the police was obviously the sensible thing to do,' said Philip.

'Unfortunately they may be delayed getting to the camp. The patrol car is engaged on some other duty,' Noel said.

'You did not actually see any damage to property, or violence?' queried Heinrich.

'No, but there is always the possibility.'

'It's a wonder Fr Kearney isn't there,' said Carmel.

'He has gone to the wedding,' said Noel. 'A boy from the camp was getting married today. Fr Kearney would be expected to put in an appearance at the reception. The travellers can be sensitive about such matters.'

Noel slowly rose from the armchair.

'Mr Fitzharris, you're surely not leaving already?' said Carmel, springing to her feet as if preparing to restrain him forcibly.

'I must get back to the camp.'

'But what can you do there?' Heinrich asked.

'Probably very little,' Noel replied, buttoning his coat. 'Again, I beg your pardon for the inconvenience occasioned by my intrusion. I can see myself out.'

'Oh, no you can't,' Carmel exclaimed. 'I'm coming with you.'

'I assure you...'

'I mean, I will accompany you to the camp.'

Heinrich swung around to face his wife. 'Carmel, you cannot go there.'

'Don't you see?' she interjected, placing a hand on his arm. 'I shouldn't have signed the petition. Heinrich, you were right.'

Heinrich did see: theoretically, at any rate, he agreed with Carmel's concept of personal responsibility, but within strict limits. It was the corollary that disturbed him—the necessity of penance, of personal reparation. What reparation could he make? How? To whom? Carmel, her upturned face young in the soft light, smiled at him, for him.

'I shall go with you,' he said.

'I knew you'd understand.' Carmel softly squeezed his arm.

Heinrich looked away from Carmel, feeling as though he were an imposter. With a sense of self-contempt, he suspected that the real reason for his decision was the presence of Philip and Mr Fitzharris, who would undoubtedly think poorly of him if he stayed at home while his wife went to the camp. That he should be held in good opinion by Mr Fitzharris, whom initially he had regarded as a somewhat comical figure and towards whom he had had a pang of resentment for being the bearer of unsettling tidings, had suddenly become important to Heinrich, and he made a mental note to cultivate his friendship. Mr Fitzharris's furrowed brow had, to Heinrich's eyes, a fertile aspect.

'Philip, I should appreciate if you would remain here for a while,' said Heinrich, arranging turfsods on the fire. 'When Eamonn comes down—he probably intends going to town—you need not say where we have gone. Just say we had to go out for a couple of minutes. Anyway, that is more or less the truth. I expect we shall be back shortly.'

'Be glad to,' said Philip, 'but listen, old man, don't you think it's unwise of you in particular to go to the camp?'

'Why do you say that?'

Philip glanced towards the door. Lowering his voice, he said, 'Because this seems to me to be an entirely Irish affair.'

Chapter 20

The fecking tinkers won't know what hit them, mused Joe Murphy, chuckling as he helped to hitch a caravan to the tractor. 'Drive on!' he shouted. The tractor's powerful diesel engine hawked and belched black smoke from its upright exhaust-pipe, as if in contempt at being asked to haul such a flimsy contrivance. The engine subsided to an effortless ticking, and tractor and caravan made a wide U-turn, halting on the opposite side of the road, facing the town.

It had occurred to Joe that he was engaged in, indeed directing, an illegality, but he believed that the police would be unlikely to exert themselves on behalf of tinkers. Furthermore, though their exchange of heated words on Thursday morning following the intrusion of animals into Joe's garden might have indicated the contrary, he and the garda superintendent were golfing friends. Anyway, Joe reasoned, no real damage was being done, and risks were minimised. Nevertheless, his heartbeat quickened each time headlamps approached from the direction of the town. As for the itinerants, he was certain that they wouldn't return until next day at earliest. Still, the sooner the operation was over the better. He hurried across the road to where four men were unhooking the caravan from the tractor.

The tractor moved forward, transferring on to the men the weight of the caravan. They held its drawing-bar, two on each side. Grunting, they lowered the drawing-bar to the ground, letting it slip the final few inches. Inside the caravan, crockery rattled.

'We have only five to go after this,' said Joe, who, especially for the occasion, had resurrected an overcoat of a colour that almost matched the smears of grease on his nose and right cheek.

'There'll be plenty of time for a few pints. We've earned them,' said Jim Walsh, stepping away from the caravan and wiping his hands on his donkey-jacket.

Joe glanced at his watch. About a minute short of a quarter to nine. As agreed that afternoon, they had assembled outside Helen Moran's house at half-past seven. His concern that an insufficient number of volunteers would turn up had proved to be unfounded: there was a surfeit, including some women, and in the past half-hour or so, more people, mostly youths, had arrived on the scene.

Apart from an attempt at interference by that silly old fool Fitzharris —he had been quickly told where to get off, though, in Joe's opinion, the language used had been a bit too enthusiastic—the operation was going smoothly, and if their luck held, the camp would shortly be completely empty of caravans.

Joe was as engrossed as a general in a crucial battle, so much so that he didn't notice the departure of Councillor Lehane.

Councillor Lehane judged it prudent to withdraw from the camp after seeing bottles passing from hand to hand and hearing voices coarsely contending with one another in bravado. Should trouble erupt, he could afterwards truthfully assert that he hadn't been present at the time, and that, if he had been, he would have done everything in his capacity as a responsible public representative to avert it. In any case, he was certain that he'd been at the scene long enough to have earned the gratitude of River Road residents. Thus, he was confident of having the best of both worlds.

The tail-lights of Councillor Lehane's Mini were merging with the lights of Fernboro when Heinrich and Carmel Obermeyer, accompanied by Noel Fitzharris, emerged from the avenue of their home. Nearby was a man with a torch, one of the traffic directors, who perhaps bored by his assignment—traffic was scarce—seemed to welcome the prospect of company and greeted them with a cheery 'Good night'.

'What's happening?' Carmel asked.

'We're getting rid of the knackers,' the man replied, as if surprised that such an activity should need to be explained.

They walked towards the camp, Carmel between Heinrich and Noel, towards the caravans lined up close to the hedge on the southern side of the road. Each caravan was tilted on to its drawing-bar.

'That fucker is back again,' said Jim Walsh.

'Who?' said Joe.

'Bushy eyebrows. Fitzharris. He has people with him.'

Joe sighted along Jim's index finger.

'Will I get some of the lads to have a word with them?'

'No, no,' Joe said hastily. Then, after checking that another caravan was firmly secured to the tractor, he issued the command for the umpteenth time. 'Drive on!'

The Obermeyers and Noel could smell the tractor's pungent diesel fumes, and in the rays of its headlamps, slicing through the camp, they saw figures, singly and in groups, some of whom were waving what appeared to be clubs. Illuminated, too, were horses tethered to a fence. They shied from the tractor and their neighs and snorts were audible over the engine.

'What are those fellows waving?' Heinrich enquired.

'Hurleys,' Noel Fitzharris said. 'The implements of our national game.'

Heinrich tucked Carmel's arm to his side, and because of her presence winced inwardly at the oaths percolating through the night. Not that the oaths were threatening; at least they weren't to his ears. While regrettable, such language was, he reflected, unconsciously habitual in many cases, an integral part of vocabulary, robbed of venom by the soft Fernboro accent. His overall feeling was one of relief. Apart from the glimpse of the hurley-carrying figures, he had witnessed nothing to justify his earlier apprehension. Though deplorable, the scene at the camp was, in the final analysis, a relatively minor incident.

The moon escaped from a cloud, outlining to Heinrich the mound-shaped tent from which, five or six weeks previously, he had seen a half-naked child, Mary McCarthy's sister, materialising. They heard an ear-splitting, primeval yowl. Laughter followed, and a dog—the shaggy greyhound—streaked past Heinrich and Carmel, tail between its legs. Up the road the dog fled, round the bend.

'You can be proud of yourselves, tormenting a dumb animal,' Carmel cried.

Bill Sullivan emerged from behind one of the four caravans that still constituted the camp and, hands thrust into the deep square-cut pockets of his jacket, cap squeezed on to his curly hair, walked towards the Obermeyers. Reaching them, he said, 'I'm sorry about the dog. There's a few troublemakers around. Some of them aren't from this area at all. I even had to stop one fellow from lighting a bale of hay.'

'None of you has any right to be here,' Carmel flared, disengaging her arm from Heinrich, as though requiring space to expend her indignation. 'What you are doing is an absolute disgrace.'

'Carmel, let us not blame this young man for…'

'No, Mr Obermeyer, your wife is right,' Bill interjected. 'The whole thing has got out of hand. I never thought things would go this far, but you know how it is. You get carried along. Don't get me wrong. I'm not defending the tinkers but what we are doing is kind of sneaky, cowardly, really. The worst thing is that most of the dirty work is being left to us, the fellows from Tuohy Place. Apart from Joe Murphy and one or two others, you don't see many here from River View Drive and the bungalows down the road.'

The headlights of the tractor transfixed Bill and the Obermeyers as it reversed into the camp, up to a caravan. Bill welcomed the interruption, for suddenly he had a sense of embarrassment at his volubility towards people with whom he was scarcely acquainted. He was ashamed of having sounded off in such a fashion: he had let himself down. He firmed down his cap.

Something to Heinrich's right gleamed in the tractor lights and caught his eye: three pointed blades, steel-cold, bright, poised, it seemed to him, to stab the earth.

'That is not scrap, surely. What is it doing here?' he said, pointing.

'The three-sod plough? That is going to be used when the camp is clear of caravans,' said Bill. 'You see, if a bit of the camp is ploughed up, the knackers'll hardly move in again.'

'Who owns the tractor and plough?' Carmel asked angrily.

'Bill was genuinely surprised. 'I thought you knew,' he said. 'It's Peter Ahern, your brother.'

Carmel had heard Peter complaining that hay was stolen from him, but she never thought he would go this far. Anger at boiling point, she made a movement towards the tractor. Expletives exploded in its vicinity and Heinrich gripped her arm. Then into view, from behind the tractor, came Noel Fitzharris, his hat and long coat making it seem as if he were stepping out of an old photograph.

'Mr Fitzharris, are you all right?' Carmel called anxiously.

'I was endeavouring to reason with them,' Noel explained as he rejoined the Obermeyers. He looked around. If only there were somewhere to sit down. If only the police were here. The tractor completed a U-turn.

———

Glass, shattering, hit the air. A caravan (one of the camp's remaining trio), as though it were mortally wounded, emitted a whooshing sound, an expiration.

———

'We'll ramble out to the camp,' said Garda Keogh, stubbing a cigarette on the dashboard ashtray.

'Whatever you say,' said Garda Breen, turning the ignition key.

His partner's compliant tone pleased Garda Keogh. It was always the same, he decided. Young fellows were starry-eyed when they joined the force, but the job wasn't long knocking some sense into them. Of course, there were exceptions, thankfully rare. Detective Prendergast, for instance. Mouthing about the law while the knackers went scot-free after robbing Mrs Moran.

Pulling out of a lay-by, the patrol car steered east for Fernboro, two miles away.

Half an hour earlier, the police station orderly had logged Gardai Keogh and Breen, who were checking in after completing a patrol, to investigate two matters: a traffic accident and a telephoned report of unusual activity at the itinerant camp. Garda Keogh allotted priority to the traffic accident which, as he had surmised, transpired to be a minor collision, requiring only a few minutes' attention. He had then directed his partner to the lay-by, where he enjoyed a leisurely smoke.

They should be nearly finished by now, thought Garda Keogh. The telephone call about the camp hadn't surprised him. He was aware of what was happening there, but kept the knowledge to himself. Little happened in and around Fernboro that he didn't know. He was counting on being presented with a *fait accompli*, a camp denuded of caravans. Where the knackers went was up to themselves, provided it was out of Fernboro police district.

Ah, the ould dog for the hard road. Garda Keogh smiled. The traffic accident covered his tracks. After all, how could he have known that the accident would turn out to be so inconsequential?. There could conceivably have been injuries, road-blocking wrecks, even fatalities. No, no one could criticise him for giving it priority. Only one person could land him in the soup. Punching Garda Breen lightly on the shoulder, he said brightly, 'Partner, what would you say to a breast of chicken?'

'I could eat the steering wheel,' said Garda Breen, dimming the headlamps on the town's outskirts.

'When we come back from the camp, pull up at Dino's. It'll be my treat,' Garda Keogh said. Then, casually, 'By the way, as far as anyone else is concerned, we didn't stop in the lay-by.'

'I won't say anything about it.' There was an indignant note in Garda Breen's voice.

Flames shot from the caravan and reached for the heavens. Screams vented terror, sense-scalding screams.

Mary McCarthy had been in near-despair about Ann's coughing and wheezing. Ann's chest was at her again. She was too sick to go to the wedding, and someone had to stay behind to mind her. Mary didn't volunteer for the task; her mother, Maggie, imposed it on her.

The occasional cawing of crows and whish of passing traffic, in Mary's ears, served only to intensify the strange silence that descended on the camp after the departure of the vans. It seemed to her that even the dogs and tethered horses and donkeys were unnaturally quiet.

In the caravan she spread on a bed-settee the ensemble which, in a large, low-price department store in Cork, she had acquired for the wedding: a long-sleeved green frock, cross-shaped gold-gloss earrings, shiny white shoes. In doing so she indulged a feeling of martyrdom, with the added intention of demonstrating to Ann the sacrifice that was being made on her behalf. Ann lay on the settee, with tousled ebony hair and febrile-bright brown eyes in a flushed face peeping over blankets. Mary was irritated at her sister, as though she had deliberately embraced illness, yet, simultaneously, she was concerned for the child.

The novelty of having sole control of the caravan gradually helped to reconcile Mary to her fate, as did the radio-recorder which her sister-in-law, Bridgie, in a gesture of sympathy, had loaned her. Mary rooted in cupboards, seeking nothing in particular: she was curious and it was a way of passing the time. Then, joyfully, she unearthed six half-pint bottles of stout, and for a while her mood verged on contentment.

Still, at frequent intervals, she would ask herself, I wonder what they're doing now, and she would self-pityingly visualise the wedding revelry; but it was a whimsically agreeable self-pity. The stout necessitated a few trips behind the hedge; otherwise she ventured out only to fetch wood for the stove. Once, she heard a car slowing down and, thinking it was about to stop, she looked out a window and saw its occupants peering at the camp, but she quickly forgot the incident. In her experience, most of the quality either passed the camp as if it were non-existent, or gawked at it, and she could never decide which of the two modes of behaviour was the more insulting.

Ann would have nothing but lemonade which Mary heated on a gas-ring. To mark the importance of the day, the McCarthys had breakfasted on a big fry-up. Mary had contemplated boycotting the meal in protest at her impending exclusion from the wedding, but her willpower was unequal to it. The breakfast fortified her for hours, until darkness was encroaching, when she peckishly consumed more than half an iced fruitcake that she washed down with her last bottle of stout. The cake was 'a treat' from her mother, who that morning had specially dispatched one of the children to purchase it.

The stout induced drowsiness in Mary. In any case, excited about the wedding, she had slept fitfully the previous night. She removed her jumper—she was in her stockinged feet—and, too lethargic to undress any further, she slid in beside Ann on the bed-settee.

Flame-painted on the night, faces were for a split-second cast into fixity.

Eamonn Obermeyer had showered and spruced himself up for his habitual Saturday night saunter into town when he noticed a glow in the landing window. He looked out. In the foreground, exposed in the moonlight, were beech trees to which shrivelled leaves clung precariously; behind the beech trees were conifers that merged into an opaque mass, and over this mass leaped a flame. Eamonn rushed down the stairs.

Victory was Joe Murphy's: never again would itinerants camp on River Road. But the fact of victory hadn't yet penetrated his mind. His face was pale, a grease-stained canvas, and his eyes were hypnotically focused on the blaze. He was unaware of the approaching car with the sign on top.

The patrol car had travelled only a short distance up River Road when Garda Keogh saw the flames.

'Good Jasus!' he exclaimed. 'Step on it!'

Garda Breen, torn from his mental savouring of crisped chicken, pressed the pedal to the floor and flicked a switch that set spinning the blue beacon on the car roof.

Heinrich uttered the word, 'Gas', and then began to run.

Alongside the caravan, tubed to it, was a cylinder. A bright yellow cylinder.

Carmel tried to follow Heinrich but was held back by Bill Sullivan.

The audience, thrillingly appalled, was tumbling into the front row.

A horse wrenched loose from its halter and bolted for freedom.

In asterisks of sparks the caravan door yielded to Heinrich's shoulder and he disappeared from view. The screams ceased. Into the vacuum of silence crackled the fire.

The blotter of night smudged the asterisks.

FICTION *from* WOLFHOUND PRESS

Death by Design
Vincent Banville

John Blaine is Dublin's very own detective!
Up to his tonsils in corpses, conmen and 'cute hoors', Blaine refuses to quit. His wife has left him, a major city gangster is searching for him — but he owes his client. The wealthy Mrs Walsh-Overman has hired him to find her son Redmond, suspected of living as a tramp in the backstreets. Has he, like several city tramps, been murdered too? £4.99

Drinker at the Spring of Kardaki
Linda McNamara

'I laughed suddenly, thinking that if I told my doctor about it all, he would merely say that my hormones were out of order. Then I shivered, clenching his fingers again, willing him to answer my call. The past was coming back to me, the hidden places of the island beckoned to me with a force I could not resist. He had begun it, with his insistence on the island, the town, even the very spring.'
Tom is curious to see the Greek island where his wife holidayed before he married her — but the monsters of the past lumber forth into the sunlight and start their roaming search among the lush grottoes and pagan rocks of the land of Jason and Medea. It seems as if only one of the couple will survive the hunt and return home.
Wonderful tales of foreign lands. The unreality of life on the move is evoked in these travellers tales, with skilful and exotic language. £5.99

Daughter of the Boyne
Patricia McDowell

Étaín, the Horserider, the most beautiful of women, is Daughter of the Boyne. Sought by Midhir as his lover and wife, she becomes the victim of many men's greed for possession and power, and of women's envy and jealousy.

This is a story of fabulous wealth and of wretched slavery, of war and magic, lust and love, and of an epic game. Through it all, just as the river nourishes the warrior kingdoms of the Boyne, so the spirits of Étaín and Midhir shape the dreams and lives of the people who inhabit the mounds and raths from Tara and the Boyne to Slievenamon.

They are shape-changers and legends in a world of wonder, magic and reality ... £4.99

On Borrowed Ground
Hugh FitzGerald Ryan

Most of all he wondered about Kate Sheehy ... As a child, she challenged the Brehony's ownership of the hill. As a folk-singer, her songs spoke of the tragic romance of the dispossessed. Jamie Nugent finds little romance in his recollections of cold linoleum and over-boiled cabbage.

On Borrowed Ground is a tale of wry humour, of cynicism and hope, a tale of the heady days of the 'fifties and of the memorable characters who peopled them.
£4.99 paperback / £10.95 hardback.